BEST SPINE

CHILLING STORIES OF ALL TIMES

SHRADDHA VERMA

TRUE SIGN
PUBLISHING HOUSE

Published by True Sign Publishing House

Address: G-3, HDB Arcade, Door Sanchar Nagar, Gulmohar,
Near UCO Bank, Bhopal, Madhya Pradesh - 462039
E-mail: truesignbooks@gmail.com
Website: www.truesign.in

Best Spine-Chilling Stories of all Times

Author: Shraddha Verma

ISBN: 978-81-19203-04-8

First Edition: 2025

CONTENTS

THRILLER AND HORROR STORIES

Introduction

Suspense is a crucial ingredient in the making of horror and thriller stories. The significance of suspense in a horror story is to bring out a twist or anunexpected moment of realization that makes someone scream and one's heart race.

Suspense and tension are key components to the horror making process. The best way to create these things is to have characters you love and making choices you hate. When you see a beloved character about to step towards the closet where the unseen serial killer is hiding, your sphincter tightens so hard it could break someone's finger.

Here are some ghost and thriller-based stories which are based on fiction and also reality but only the purpose of this book is to give enjoyment and knowledge about such incidents which have taken place in the various parts of the world.

Let's enjoy by reading them.

SCARY MANSION

You must have heard stories of many haunted mansions till now. But there was no mansion where anyone lived. That's why the story is so true. And how many lies. This doubt was always there. But the mansion whose story we are telling you today, is about a family who lives there. And Ramiya lives together for whom two hundred years have passed since his death.

If the pages of time are taken into account, then the story is almost two hundred years old. There is a haveli near Etah in Uttar Pradesh. It is not deserted but is inhabited from members of a family that is devastated by a soul. Yes, life and death live side by side in this mansion.

If the decision is taken in view of the accidents, then here death is very heavy on life. One Ramiya has taken the lives of many people till now. That Ramiya was a courtesan, who used to be famous. But two brothers staked their claim on it.

Three friends, drunken car-o-bar, the horrifying story of a murderer standing in the middle of the river at 2 am. Story: Mystery of 10 pieces of dead body revealed with 500 fridges and 1000 mobile numbers!

Dirty eye on 'daughter-in-law' and the whole story of Anjan Das murder hidden in live-in relationships These proofs can get Aftab execute!

There was a fight while watching the dance. Then the quarrel started. And then a death was the sign of what happened in this quarrel. That Ramiya was killed in a quarrel. This story is from 200 years ago. But even today she is seen in the same mansion. Dance songs with the sound of ghungroos. People live in mansions... but in the midst of fear. Many untimely deaths have happened.

SCREAMS COME FROM THIS MANSION FOR MANY YEARS

The story begins on one day. That day he was offering his last salaam to Suraj. It was dusk when suddenly a scream echoed from this mansion in Etah's Chamkari village. The voice is of a girl... she says... don't take me out of the mansion... this is my house... otherwise I I will ruin you all. Before anyone understands anything, another scream echoes.

But this time the pain of death is also mixed in the scream. Water... water...some girl begs for water with a moaning sound...had this incident happened somewhere else...maybe someone would have come to help... but in this village everyone is afraid One gets scared... because for the last several decades, such screams... have been coming out from this mansion... and people have been tremblingly waiting for the morning...

The owner of this mansion, Satendra Tomar, says that earlier everything was fine here. But gradually this problem kept on increasing. Here the sound of ghungroos was heard..the sounds of dancing...this way the problem kept getting created. The magicians were called. Sometimes there would be voices...you will have to leave the house...this is my house. In this way we started getting scared.

We started living in the shadow of fear. But the question was who is this girl. .And what is its relation with this house... why as soon as the day sets... the silence like a graveyard spreads on the roads passing by this mansion... and with a strange reluctance the girl is seen wandering in this mansion Sometimes peeping through the window, sometimes gazing from the roof of the haveli, waiting for some traveler from far away... who has seen her carefully...

It is said that his eyes seem to pierce the heart like a spear. But once upon a time people were crazy about these eyes. People wanted to see her by standing around where she used to stand. People's eyes kept gazing at the window of the house where she used to live. People used to wait... that when the window would open and she would be seen... Such was the charm of Ramiya...

SUCH A MANSION IN WHICH BOTH LIFE AND DEATH RESIDE

The elders living around this mansion tell that a beautiful girl used to emerge from this mansion. The one whom he used to try to catch.. she used to become a cat. Today, both life and death reside in this kothi. They are not empty like other havelis.

The soul of the courtesan Ramiya of the past also resides here, And the owner of this kothi too. But what happens to these lives that are constantly breathing in the shadow of death. It is enough to tell that many people have died because this haveli has lost many loved ones till now. The extent is that even the children of this haveli have started thinking before doing mischief or chirping.

All the lives that are left in this mansion today... there is no trace of life on their faces... a beautiful but terrifying face is constantly visible to them... staring blankly... perhaps asking

INSIDE (EG IN THE HOUSE, IN THE BILL)

MAT comes... a beautiful but terrifying face is constantly visible to them... staring in a daze... probably asking what courage is left even after the death of so many people. To stay here...but why is Ramiya burning in the fire of revenge....why doesn't she feel pity even on innocent children...what happened to her..

WHO WAS RAMIYA BAI AFTER ALL?

Ramiya Bai... When her anklet used to sparkle.... then people used to go crazy... The owner of every haveli used to dream that one day these anklets would be tinkled only for him... two hundred years ago Ramiya used to perform mujra in this haveli... In the list of fans of Ramiya, the names of two real brothers of this area are also there.

Shamar Daya Karna who was almost every evening at Rasi's

Used to count... used to spend almost every evening with him...

But Ramiya was the name of that bull, whose beauty and talent, what relationships and relationships... used to get scattered in a moment... and the same happened with those two brothers too... both of them were so emotional about Ramiya that, they have become enemies of each other's life.

And when Ramiya tried to control the uncontrollable situation madness became his fault

She wanted that there should be no bloodshed between the two. But exactly the opposite happened. There was blood but not of those two brothers but of Ramiya. Who had no fault. If there was any fault, it was of her beauty. The fault was his passion. And the fault was that of her flabby waist and boisterous gait.

On which even people from a distance of seven miles were pulled and used to come But today two brothers broke up on the same beauty. that they clashed with each other and the dagger entered Ramiya's chest Gone. That dagger had left a deep wound. ... of life

The breath scattered like the curls of her broken anklet

Was going... death had knocked...

And then dancing, singing, masti chitholi along with Ramiya, everything was over with her death. And this death was very heavy on this haveli.. Time passed but her memories never got blurred...how could it have been.... because Ramiya had not left this haveli at all. It is still visible to people today.

But she doesn't sing and hum... roaming around in a frenzy...reminiscing those golden days. When one party doesn't arise, people desperate to decorate another reach there....the only difference is that two hundred years ago, every step that came out of this hall was swinging with joy...but today dead bodies come out from here. ...

Even today the shadow of those who died here is visible.

Haveli owner Satendra Tomar tells about this that one day my mother saw a shadow. After this he had died. In this way, Ramiya's wrath has always cast a shadow on our mansion. My three children have died one by one. Then my wife has also lost her life.

However, now the responsibility of saving this mansion is on Satendra. He is an educated person. And earlier he didn't even believe in things like ghosts... but today when he looks at his family.. then every relationship seems incomplete... he is alive.. but his wife is no more.. If someone is alive... then mother is dead... sister-in-law is there.... but brother is dead.

It is said that before the Tomar family, the Gupta family used to live in this mansion. The frequent deaths broke the Gupta family so much.... that they sold this mansion for a pittance... Tomar family bought it... and as soon as they bought it...

Eight people, old and young, died one by one.... then took support.... of worship... the result... this time the one who had done the worship lost his life.

EVEN TODAY THERE IS NO BRIGHTNESS IN THE MANSION

What does the old lady think about this mansion? About this, the old mistress Omwati Gupta tells that there is Chamkari village situated on

Agra road. Weaving the moments of time, almost two hundred years have passed today.

Almost two hundred years have passed while weaving, but nothing new happened here after that incident.

Except the story of Ramiya, which is woven into the fabric here. Some with such intensity that it is also visible. Unmani c...wandering...outside the haveli.. and inside too...as a result its owners thought it better to sell it.

This is the reason why today there is no brightness on anyone's face in this mansion... Children live in a dark place. Elders..as if..they are alive... the house doesn't feel like home....and how can they feel because the house has never adopted them...but it is sure...to all their near and dear ones.. .. suddenly...

What is the truth of Ramiya.. We can't say... Yes, we can definitely say that there have been countless unnecessary deaths in both the families living here... And if all this is a coincidence then it is definitely a very scary coincidence.. Perhaps more terrifying than the fear of Ramiya.

ELIZABETH BATHORY

This is a heart-wrenching real story of a small country in Europe from the Kingdom of Hungary. This is a very old country which was once a part of the Roman Empire. It is said that this country was attacked by a group of species called Hans. From that time its name became Hungarian. This is a country where parents cannot name a child. Rather, the government takes out a list and the parents name their child out of that.

This story of this Hungarian country is many decades old. This story is from 1558 to 1610. At that time there was a Hungarian Empire. The king of this kingdom was King Matthias-II. The Bathory family was associated with this empire. This Bathory family was also a part of the royal family. Because in this family there used to be the biggest warriors to protect Hungary.

FERENC NADSDY

Ferenc Nadsdy was a warrior of this family who proved to be the hero of Hungary in the war with the Turks. Because of this, this family used to live in a big palace. And no ordinary citizen of Hungary could refuse the order that came from this palace.

Elizabeth Bathory was the wife of Ferenc Nádsdy, a warrior of the royal family Bathory who was very beautiful and whose beauty used to be discussed. An order from Elizabeth and there used to be a line of servants in the palace. But this Elizabeth Bathory became so proud of her beauty that when someone told her that she was getting old now, she got angry.

She used to get angry just because of this. She used to believe in vampires and didn't know how many such books in which there were talks of killing humans to fulfill their wishes. I had heard it being said from someone's mouth that once a princess bathed in the blood of virgins, she always remained young and beautiful. Just because of these things, Elizabeth Bathory became infatuated. Now she started thinking that if she bathed in the fresh blood of virgin girls, she would remain young forever.

Just to fulfill this craze, she herself became a devil. Now in her palace she started fulfilling her whims with the help of three servants. For this, she initially targeted those girls who were from poor families.

The age of those girls was around 16 years. Those poor virgin girls were called to work in the palace. They never got a chance to go out again. Now this Bathory family had a direct relation with the Hungarian Empire, so no one had the courage to question it. The second thing was also that poor girls used to get work. But it was not known that those girls were subjected to horrific torture in that palace.

They were burned with a hot iron, and the flesh of the face and breast were scraped

Who was Elizabeth Bathory Serial Killer:

It is said that Elizabeth Bathory used to make virgin girls her victims even when her husband was alive. But in the year 1604, after the death of her husband Ferenc Nadsdy, she became a complete devil. Now she had started torturing in such a way that people's souls used to tremble after knowing it. Elizabeth Bathory had made her palace in Chaschis, Slovenia, a palace of death.

It is said that before the death of her husband, she used to bathe in the same blood after killing virgin girls. But after the death of her husband, she hated the delicate organs of the girls so much that she used to torture them before killing them. The girls were tied with chains and used to burn their hands and feet with hot iron.

Sometimes she herself used to bite their face and breast with her teeth. If a girl's nails looked good, she used to uproot them. Many times she used to pour ice water on the body without clothes and sometimes she used to leave their bare body in the cold. Many times she used to apply honey on their body. So that insects could bite them badly. If a girl was beautiful, then she used to cut her breast and face and remove the pieces of flesh.

It is also claimed that Elizabeth Bathory used to cut the delicate parts of girls with scissors. Many times she used to cut the private part also with scissors. Even more frightening and cruelly, she tortured which we cannot write in words.

AFTER ALL, HOW DID ELIZABETH BATHORY'S CREEPY SECRET COME TO LIGHT?

Actually, Elizabeth Bathory used to invite only girls from poor families to the palace. But those girls never returned home again. In this way, gradually the number of girls started decreasing. Seeing this, Elizabeth started ordering the girls of rich families to come to the palace.

Now when even the girls of rich families could not return home, people started getting suspicious. Meanwhile, there were some girls who somehow escaped Elizabeth's torture and came out of the palace.

After listening to their plight, the people of the rich family complained about it to the Hungarian King. When this was known, the poor people of the village also showed courage and complained to the Hungarian King Matthias-II. The Hungarian King took it seriously and got his very special officer to investigate into the matter.

650 MURDERS IN 20 YEARS, INVESTIGATION CLAIMED ONLY 80 DEATHS

The investigation started in the year 1610. In this the tortures were confirmed. When seen in the palace of Elizabeth Bathory, many secret rooms were made torture houses there. In the palace, the dead bodies of the girls were tied with fetters. Many of these girls were alive, while many had died in agony.

Elizabeth Bathory and her three servants were arrested by the royal army from the spot. Now all the three servants were hanged for this heart-wrenching incident. But this did not happen with Elizabeth, because she belonged to the royal family. That's why she was punished to be kept locked in a room for life. She breathed his last on 21 August, 1614 in the same room. In this way, after 4 years of arrest in 1610, she died.

It is said about Elizabeth Bathory that she tortured and killed more than 650 virgin girls in 20 years from 1590 to 1610. After killing these girls, she used to bathe in the bathtub for hours after taking out their blood.

However, in the investigation ordered by the Hungarian King, it was claimed that only 80 girls were murdered. Many books and films have also been made on Elizabeth Bathory. It is said that she was the world's most dreaded female serial killer ...

OWEN TOMKINSON

Here is someone who wanders everyday in this cemetery...with his desires...stick in hand and hat on his head...this strange dress because he was an Englishman... He has died about a hundred years ago...but there are wishes that even after death it does not let it die..

This is the untold story of Bihar's Gaya city...the area is Iqbal Nagar... and the soul which often used to meet people two to four for its small desire, its name used to be, **OWEN TOMKINSON...AN ENGLISH OFFICER.**

The one who died in the year 1906...but even today...even after passing of more than 115 years...he is wandering...it may sound strange but this soul needs only this. .tea and biscuit...and he is seen walking in this whole area every night with this desire of his...

Coming in front of a spirit and asking for tea, biscuits or cake puts one in awe...but there are many witnesses of this strange desire of that powerful spirit...it is also true that the graveyard from which that spirit comes. Most of the graves there are of small children...

So is it to be believed that this English family, who was victim of an accident, does this to fulfill the unfulfilled wish of one of their children... It is difficult to decide, but it is true that if that Englishman ordered... either he has to give tea biscuits..or he has to promise to deliver in the morning...only then it is possible to get rid of him..

People are scared of this unique wish of Owen Tomkinson's soul...but it is not as if life has stopped...because it is possible for anyone to fulfill this small wish...this also happened that efforts were also made to keep this soul within its limits...

But this spirit started appearing again after some time...with the same desire...tea and biscuits...after all, why does that soul do this...

what is the story behind it....this is such a question who is wandering in this whole area for the last one century in search of his answer like that soul...

Who was Owen Tomkinson who is not at peace in his grave even after 100 years of his death... Why does he make strange requests like tea, cake and biscuits to the passers by... No one knows.. .History only tells that he was a British soldier and was stationed here... It is about 1906 when cholera suddenly spread here and 47 year old Owen fell in its grip on 19 September 1906...

And this is where he got his grave... time passed, British rule passed... but this soldier of that rule roams here even today... with his unique desire... people of Iqbal Nagar tell that till a few years back. So Owen's spirit often used to stand blocking the way in the silence of the night....and used to leave only when he was presented with a treat of tea and biscuits......

Owain was definitely freed after the sticks were removed, but call it the power of those beggars that there was some control on his actions....but he kept on appearing again and again suddenly and people fulfilled his wishes even if they didn't want to. Well...the surprising thing in this whole sentence is that even if people fear him...but no one can be found here who hates him....

This is a strange country...it accepts only those people who live with it for a long time...does not even look at souls with hatred...everybody says that the soul only asks for tea and biscuits. ..doesn't harm anyone...

This cemetery of Gaya's Iqbal Nagar is actually so unique that there is a different feeling just by stepping here... Be it the carving done on the tombs here or the architecture of the tombs... There is no such thing in the country. There will not be another graveyard whose tomb top, despite being made of stone, rotates like an umbrella and emits strange sounds...

IS THIS A REASON BEHIND THE STORY OF FEAR?

Although, amidst all these surprises, the life of Iqbal Nagar has learned to live with the spirit of Owen. Even now they go through the same path... although in their heart they definitely celebrate...that they should not face Owen again...it is also true

No matter how simple the soul may be... it is a soul... this strange story of Owen... shocks even some educated people... they do not believe that there is such a soul... and their The basis of this argument is that of a unique wish related to Owen... in which he says give me tea and biscuits...

Psychologists believe that if without checking the reality of any story, it is given air...that story slowly starts to appear like reality...and the minds of the simple people of the village force them to consider even the rope as a snake. Does...

The graveyard to which this dreadful spirit is related is actually out of use now... The Christian community has kept away from here for the past many decades... There are also people around here who have been living here for a long time and this dreadful coincidence never happened in his life.

But along with such people, there are some other people who have not only seen Owen's soul but also shook hands with him... Why are they becoming a part of this rumor when they are not going to get any benefit from it. ...

There is a community in Iqbal Nagar which has not met Owen's soul, but they have no doubt about its existence.

However, along with the psychologists, the Christian community here also declares all these things as empty stories... Some people even say in a low voice that some land mafias are eyeing this three and a half acres of cemetery land and all these Somewhere behind the stories he has a hand too.

But in spite of knowing all this, all the people have been wearing the cloak of faith in Owen's spirit and his desire for a long time...and before Owen would make any request to them...they themselves would appear at this grave. Have...with...tea, biscuit or cake...

MYSTERIOUS CAVE

No matter how many revolutions science may make, but even today there are some such secrets, some such places which neither man nor science has been able to reveal. There are some places on earth where no one could return till date, no one could know where people got lost, so till date no one dared to go there, because there is only one meaning to go there, by oneself.

This place is the most mysterious cave in the world, whose secret is not only unsolved, but also unknown, this most mysterious cave inside the underworld is also considered to be the oldest cave of human civilization, built in the Yucatan peninsula of Mexico (Mexico) inside the underworld. The mention of this cave is also found in the texts of Mayan civilization.

It is as scary as it is from outside, it is as shocking as it is from inside, the story of this cave has been heard and narrated for centuries, but till date no one has been able to know its secret, there are many other caves inside the cave whose depth no one knows how much it is, and the stories that are famous about this cave are heart-wrenching.

It is a belief that whoever goes deep into these caves, never comes back and dies wandering in it, many times people tried to go into these caves but either they never came back, or they returned earlier fearing its depth. Some divers even tried to find the world's largest underwater cave, but they could only go a short distance.

According to those divers, this cave found on top of Mexico's Yucatan peninsula connects two caves submerged in water, and they have discovered this secret after 14 years of hard work and hundreds of hours of diving, while not knowing how many. There are secrets that are imprisoned in this cave, scientists believe that 10,000 to 12,000 years ago these caves were used by the people of Mayan civilization.

In the texts of the Mayan civilization, this cave is called Sinot Cave, which is the Spanish form of the word **'de Zinot'** of the Mayan civilization, many signs of the Mayan civilization are found in this ten kilometer long cave. It is believed that these caves filled with fresh water are spread over a total of 1,400 square kilometers, the texture inside the cave is a sample of ancient Spanish artwork, pictures of similar artifacts are also found in the texts of Mayan civilization.

This cave is the fifth and one of the oldest caves in the world under water, the view inside the cave is surprising, the lower part of the cave is made like a common cave, but the upper part is open so that the air reaches this cave. Easily accessible, as beautiful as the upper part of the cave, its underwater world is even more fascinating.

It is said that as the depths of the water of this cave are discovered, many more of its secrets will be revealed, but in every dive here, there is a challenge for the divers to return safely, because in the caves filled with water, the path is lost or the oxygen runs out. But divers are often killed. By the way, in terms of size, the world's largest cave is in America, this cave called Mammoth Cave is 650 kilometers long.

More like a mystery, the spectacular Giant Crystal Cave is connected to the Naica Mine, located nearly 1,000ft below Chihuahua Desert, Mexico. Its main chamber contains the largest selenite crystals ever found, some of them reaching 11 meters in length, 4 meters in diameter and about 55 tons in weight. Until you notice the orange-suited men clambering around, it's hard to grasp the extraordinary scale of this underground crystal forest. These razor-sharp rocks, deadly crevasses, unbearable heat and scalding water makes this place a challenge for explorers. This cave was discovered by two brothers drilling in the Naica lead and silver mine.

SCIENCE COLLEGE

There are many such places where humans do not but ghosts and spirits live, you must have heard or seen many such places where no human wanders far and wide because the ghosts living there do not harm anyone. also doesn't allow to come. Today, we are telling you about one such haunted place in India which has been lying in ruins for years. This place is Khairatabad Science College of Hyderabad.

The Science College of Khairatabad has been closed for years and now its building looks no less than a post bungalow of a ghost film. Khairatabad Science College, which has become a ruin, was earlier counted among the brilliant science colleges here, a large number of far-flung children from other areas used to come here to study, but now it is closed, in fear of ghosts. People say that now only ghosts live here.

Neither humans nor science has been able to reveal whether there are ghosts in the college or not. Yes, it is true that earlier humans used to study here but now science is taught to ghosts here. This science college is such a place, where our powers of thinking and understanding are lost, because fear and dread starts dominating us here. A question may arise in your mind that how did this science college become a house of ghosts, so let us tell you what is the secret of this building?

History tells that earlier thousands of children used to come to study in this college, they used to roam around here all the time, it is said that when this science college was closed due to some reason, then the dead bodies kept in the lab were taken for examination. They were not disposed of, they were left there. During that time suddenly people around heard strange sounds from here, some claimed to have seen a ghost, some a witch, although none of such claims could be proved.

These rumors were enough to turn this building into ruins, fear automatically arose here, people stopped coming and going. Even the college was closed, yes but the government hired a man to guard this college and another letter of fear was written from here.

It is said that the very next day the watchman died in a strange way and his dead body was found lying in the college, the body of the watchman was found in such a way that both the fear and suspicion of the people became more confirmed, everyone started saying that the watchman had been murdered by the ghosts. Since the incident till date no one has tried to go to this college, now silence prevails here.

In this way, this college started turning into ruins in no time. Now the people here say that whoever goes to this college does not come back again. Everyone knows, science also believes that this is nothing but mental illusion, but still people live in fear, not just fear, but such places are made tourist spots and this is a very simple thing, because in our country fear is sold.

ANNALIESE HORROR STORY

Pastor said there are six ghosts in its body. Emily Rose killed in the name of exorcism

The number of such people in the world would also be in lakhs or crores only, who believe too much in what is considered to be baseless fact like ghosts, exorcism and witchcraft. Of course, many people consider it as an illusion, but there are some such stories in this world which compel us to believe in this illusion.

Things like ghosts, witchcraft, exorcism are definitely not given importance in today's time of progress. But this is such a deep-rooted reality among humans that it cannot be turned away completely.

One such incident came in front of the world about 72 years back. This is around 1951. Bavaria is a city in Germany. Annaliese Mitchell, who lived in the same city, struggled with similar miseries in her life that buried her and her family's dreams to the ground before they could come true. Because it has been claimed that all this happened because his own body had become home to not one or two but six souls.

No one can say for sure what is the truth of this shocking thing, although there are definitely eyewitnesses to what Annaliese Mitchell and her family went through. And the story narrated by those eyewitnesses and the story of what they saw and heard not only amazes but also gives goosebumps.

In fact, this story and whatever happened in the story happened in a country where science was given the most importance. Science means everything that can stand the test of logic. And whatever is not logical is considered as delusion. That is, superstition cannot find any place in any situation.

AN INCURABLE DISEASE

Exorcism: The matter of six souls in the body of a wise girl also came to the fore from the same land of Germany which gave the highest status to science. In fact, when Annaliese Mitchell was 16-years-old, a serious disease came under the grip of temporal lobe epilepsy.

The family members left no stone unturned in the treatment, yet she did not get well. Rather she started getting weaker with each passing day. This disease was such that the patient not only started losing his memory, but he also didnot have control over the movements of the body.

Annaliese Mitchell's family members were Christians, and very fanatical about their religion. He had unwavering faith in Ish. And that's why those people used to take out time from their work and also engaged in the promotion of religion.

In the company of her family members, Annaliese also felt that she too would grow up to serve the church and preach for her religion. But due to illness, the desire of his started dying slowly. The family members showed Annaliese to all kinds of doctors, got her every possible treatment done, but to no avail, but with time, her disease also increased.

AN ACT OF A GIRL AND THE ARROGANCE OF A DEMONIC SOUL

Seeing their daughter's deteriorating health, Annaliese's family then told their guru about the disease. But even they could not do anything about it. Annaliese's' health started to decline day- by-day. Rather, now she had started doing strange and poor things, seeing which the family members started getting scared.

This thing got stuck in the hearts of the family members that their daughter was not suffering from any disease, but she was possessed by some evil spirit. Realizing this illusion, Annaliese's parents decided to show it to the priest of the church. Entangled in this thought, Annaliese's parents called a person they knew, who used to work as an exorcist, to their house.

Annaliese's father came home to pick her up and took her to Annaliese's room. At that time Annaliese was not on her bed but was lying on the floor. On seeing the man who was brought home by Annaliese's father, Annaliese urinated on the floor and then started licking him with her tongue.

Apart from this, he picked up a coal lying there and started chewing it. The thing that the person noticed the most after seeing Annaliese was that while doing such an act, Annaliese had a strange smile on her face. She neither laughed openly nor cried openly but her facial expressions used to change very fast.

AND STARTED EXORCISM OF A SICK GIRL

Seeing this condition of Annaliese, he was convinced that she was not in the grip of disease but she was possessed by the devil. Then that person advised Annaliese's parents to perform an exorcism. Annaliese's parents, who were almost broken seeing their daughter's condition, could not understand anything, so they also accepted that advice and gave her the go-ahead to do the exorcism.

Then the two priests of the church arranged for the tantric activities. The most surprising thing was that while completing this action, Annaliese was tied in thick chains so that she could sit in one place. She was exorcised many times but there was no improvement in her condition rather it started getting worse with every passing moment.

Many times the exorcist priests then did their own tricks and then revealed for the first time that Annaliese's body was possessed by not one but two but six spirits. Even the priests, through their experiences and through tantra mantra, came to know the names of the spirits that had made a home in Annaliese's' body.

While the other was Judas Iscariot, the third was Ken Adam, the name of the fourth soul was Hitler. The name of the fifth soul was Valentine Fleishman and the name of the sixth soul was Lucifer.

TANTRIC RITUALS TO DRIVE AWAY SPIRITS

The priests also told that all these spirits had different roles which were not allowing Annaliese to take rest under any circumstances. It is said that when these tantric activities were done on Annaliese, the priests also had to bear its bad effects.

The most shocking aspect is that at the time when these exorcisms and tantric rituals were performed, all the chanting and all the sounds in the room were also recorded. The names of those souls could be known only through those recorded voices.

On many occasions, it was even seen that the demonic spirits inside Annaliese used to dominate so much that she used to get very angry with Annaliese's parents and the situation used to reach so far that the very weak Annaliese used to kill her parents. She used to pick it up and throw it.

At that time, there was so much strength in his grip that it was as if a powerful wrestler was holding him. And when she was chained to the bed, she used to scratch her parents or priests badly with her nails.

Things were getting so out of control that anyone was afraid to enter Annaliese's room. In such a situation, when Annaliese had no one, she started attacking and injuring herself.

In the midst of all these incidents, the priests did not stop the process of tantra kriya and exorcism, but now they started doing tantra kriya several times a day. The continuous exorcism had such an effect that suddenly Annalies'e's attitude changed and she started being happy.

She started laughing... started talking ... and started listening and telling about her past life in a good way. The family members started feeling that now the effect of exorcism had started and their daughter was now getting better.

But for the family members, these moments of happiness remained only for a few days. Because after that suddenly Annaliese stopped eating and drinking everything. And his health began to decline very rapidly.

AND ON JULY 1 SHE FELL ASLEEP FOREVER

When the priests who performed tantric asked him, he himself told the whole thing while crying that someone inside him stopped him from eating and drinking. The effect of giving up eating and drinking was that Annaliese started becoming a victim of malnutrition. His body started getting weak. The priests now intensified the process of exorcism.

On June 30, 1976, when she was exorcised for the last time at night, she told the priest that now she was completely tiredand had to get rid of this body. And saying this, Annaliese started crying badly. Seeing this condition of their daughter, Annaliese's parents also burst into tears. Even the priests who came to perform the tantric rituals had tears in their eyes.

After saying this, Annaliese fell asleep. And then she never got up. It is being told that on July 1, Annaliese took a long breath in the morning and closed her eyes forever.

After Annaliese's death, the doctors did her post-mortem and it was found that she died due to malnutrition. Then the doctors told Annaliese's parents that if she had been given medical treatment in time, she might have survived. But they chose conservative methods instead of medical treatment, so the child died.

ISLAND OF DOLLS

This is the most dreaded island in the world, where the wretchedness is visible at every step and these dolls testify to fear. You must be thinking that where did so many dolls come from on an island where not even a human lives, but the secrets of this sinful doll island do not end here. People say that a girl's soul wanders on this island and to keep the girl's soul calm, thousands of dolls have been kept here.

The tales do not end here, some people have claimed that anyone who dares to visit this island at night is killed. Because sinful Gudiya absolutely cannot tolerate anyone stepping into her kingdom. This island with sinful dolls is in Mexico and the name of this most scary island in the world is - "La Isla de las Muenecas". In English people know this island as "Island of Dolls".

Two dead bodies found in a house, and the police surrounded by suspense are witnessing murder and suicide.

SECRET OF THE ISLAND OF THE SINFUL DOLLS

The story of this island is as scary as it is interesting and mysterious. There was a time when no one used to visit this island, yes, nowadays some people have started coming here to roam , but the courage to step here at night is bigger than the biggest. Not even Surma does. Actually, behind this island is a terrible story related to these dolls.

This is about 60 years old in the 1950s. Only one person lived on this island, whose name was Julian Santana Barrera. Julian was a mystic who had renounced the world. One day while wandering, he reached this place and then started living here, he had no home and he used to live here alone. But soon Julian's life was about to go awry. One day he saw that suddenly a girl came to this island and drowned here in this canal. Julian could not save her, the girl drowned but she had a doll in her hand which Julian found. Julian claimed that since then the soul of this girl started wandering on this island.

One night, Julian had a dream of the girl who had drowned here, she told Julian that she loved her doll very much. If her doll was kept safely on this island, her spirit would never disturb anyone, after that night Julian becomes obsessed. He started decorating this island with dolls, through this canal many dolls would flow to this island and then they would remain on this island. A special place was made for each doll on this island.

WHEN WAS THE SECRET OF THIS ISLAND REVEALED?

Until 31 years ago, the world used to think that no one lived on this island, for the first time in 1990, the world came to know about this island, the dolls living here and Julian. After this, the island became the headlines of the whole world. People started coming here one by one, many people would bring some old dolls with them and leave it here. As a result, the number of dolls increased from thousands to lakhs. But now something was going to happen on this island which no one had expected. The world was thinking that the secret of this island had been revealed, but now the secret of this island was going to deepen further.

The island of dolls had become famous all over the world, people started gathering here. The fear of people about this island had gone out, but the owner of this island, Julian, always felt that only dolls had saved this island from the evil spirit. He used to believe these dolls to be alive, but people used to think that the dolls on this island had nothing to do with the soul. But one day something happened which deepened the mystery of this island.

Julian's death deepens the mystery

It is a matter of April 21, 2001. One morning Julian's dead body was found near the canal. This was the exact place where the body of the girl with the doll was found in 1950. As long as Julian lived here alone, this island was very sacred, but after 1990 people made it unholy. People think that Julian was killed by the spirit and these dolls together. It is another matter that many people do not believe it, Julian died under very mysterious circumstances. Rumors spread throughout Mexico that the island's doll and spirit were behind Julian's death. Since then till today no one goes to this island at night and those who go during the day also have a terrible feeling.

Most people are afraid to visit this island, but for the brave, this island has become a tourist spot. Hundreds of people reach here everyday through a special boat running in the canal, people leave their old dolls on this island due to which the number of dolls is increasing here everyday. Julian is no more but his relatives now take care of this island. This doll island has become so famous all over the world that UNESCO has declared it a World Heritage. What is the real secret of this island and these dolls, no one has been able to solve it, but it is certain that as long as this island remains, the stories related to it will continue to be heard and told.

52-YEAR-OLD MURDER MYSTERY

The half-burnt dead body of a woman found 52 years ago is still waiting for its full identity. A 52-year-old secret is still buried in the valley of mystery.

The 52-year-old murder mystery that has puzzled police across the world, including Norway.

That 52-year-old suspense is still suspense today. Suspense that after all who is that half-burnt Isdale women, where did she come from, for whom did she come, why did she come and the biggest question is of whose bloody conspiracy did she get lost in the deep darkness of oblivion.

WHAT IS THE IDENTITY OF THE ISDALE WOMAN?

When, why and where is that woman so hidden in this puzzle that all the smart policemen around the world lay down their weapons in front of this mystery. At least this has been happening for the last 52 years.

Science has also made a lot of progress since 52 years ago when that dead body was found. But perhaps there has not been enough progress yet to give that Isdale woman her lost identity. The corpse is still preserved

DEAD BODY LYING FACE DOWN AMONG THE ROCKS

This incident came to light on 29 November, 1970 from Norway's most dangerous and mysterious Vergen Valley. When a man saw a woman lying face down among the rocks in the Ice Valley here, known as Isdale. She also had two daughters with that man who was scared to see this scene.

When the woman lying face down on the rocks was turned over, her face and front part of the body were completely burnt. So much so that it was impossible to recognize him by looking at his burnt face.

THE CLUES CONFUSED THE MURDER

When the dead body of that half-burnt woman was further searched, some signs were found which deepened this mystery even more. For example, all the clothes on the woman's body, all the labels were removed or cut. The water bottle found with him also appeared to be without a tag and label.

The most shocking aspect was the condition in which the woman was found. Both her hands were as if a boxer was defending himself by clenching his fists. And even more shocking thing iwas that the front part of the body was charred, but there was a burnt mark on the top of the waist only.

INTENTIONALLY LEFT MURDER CLUES

At first, the Norwegian police were shocked to find the dead body. But the condition of the body and the removal of marks from the body put the Norwegian police in deep trouble.

The woman's body was found in Isdale, Norway. This is the same valley which has got the infamy of the name of Death Valley in Norway. Because many suicides used to happen in this area.

The Norwegian police, who were desperately searching for the identity of the anonymous woman, did not give any identification of the woman which was found near the dead body. What bothered the police the most was that there were no signs of a campfire or bonfire anywhere near where the woman's body was found. So how did that woman get burnt?

THE KILLER HID AFTER GIVING A CLUE

The police team also found a broken umbrella, nylon socks, plastic water bottle, a purse and blue snow-worn rubber shoes near the dead body. But there was no such tag on all these things which could tell where it all came from and how it reached here.

Police investigators were surprised to find that the woman's name and identity had been erased from everything they found. And all the things related to the woman were kept very neatly decorated on a nearby rock. Traces of petrol were also found under the place where the woman was lying.

The first thing the police do after any dead body is found is post-mortem. So the post-mortem of that dead body was done. Post=mortems usually solve the mystery. But here everything was happening in reverse. So here also the matter became more complicated.

In the post-mortem, more than 50 sleeping pills were found in the stomach of the dead body, which were not yet fully digested. Apart from this, smoke was found from her lungs which simply meant that the woman was alive at the time when she was set on fire.

There were deep injury marks on her neck, which suggested that the woman was thrown from above in a burning condition. Falling on the rock had caused fatal injury to the neck. It had been learned from the autopsy report that the cause of death was carbon monoxide as well as the effect of sleeping pills. That is, at first it seemed as if it was suicide.

SUSPENSE OF GOLD TEETH INTACT

During the same autopsy, the police were shocked by the woman's teeth, as most of the teeth were filled with gold. But that method of teeth texture and gold filling was not of Scandinavia. This meant that she was not from Norway, it meant that she was a foreigner.

After getting this basic information, the police once again went about their work and kept washing their heads over the dead body of that woman.

Three to four days passed, the police car remained stuck where it was stuck. But after three days the police got a major breakthrough when they found two suitcases from the railway station. That too unclaimed.

SECRET LOCKED IN AN OPEN SUITCASE

When the investigation started, the fingerprints of the woman from a spectacles closed in the suitcase testified that these suitcases belonged to the same woman who was no longer in this world. But the things that came out from the suitcase also confused the police.

Apart from glasses, the police found a time table, some maps, wigs used by women in both suitcases, make-up items and an eczema cream as well as clothes, currency of several countries and a notepad.

The currency was kept hidden separately in both the suitcases, which included Norwegian currency kroner, Swiss franc, Belgian franc and British pound, besides some Thai Bhat coins. Apart from this, Deutsche Mark kept hidden in the lining of a suitcase was also found.

FOUR CLUE AND FOUR THEORY:

Despite finding and knowing so much, the mystery deepened from here because the identity was erased from all the stuff.

The police still did not give up because in his hand there was such an object, which was probably a written sign of Maktool's hand, and that was a notepad with some code word written in blue ink on it.

After a long struggle, the police got success in understanding the code word written in that notepad. All these code words were in fact all the details of that woman's stay in Norway on different dates and going from there and coming there. Police accepted that according to the notepad, the mysterious woman came and stayed in Norway only according to the dates recorded. More than this the police did not get any success.

While searching for all the things found from the Isdale woman, the police finally got another success while it got the address of the shop from where the woman had taken the shoes and the shoes which helped the police to investigate. Couldn't move even a step forward. That shoe shop was found in the city of Stavanger, about 210 km from Sisa Vargan.

When the police immediately reached the shop, they came to know one more special thing about that woman. The shopkeeper's son told the policemen that this pair of shoes had been sold some time back to that attractive looking middle-aged woman with black hair.

The policemen also found it surprising that why the shopkeeper remembered that woman. So the shopkeeper said that the woman was very good at conversation, but the real reason to remember was the strange smell coming from her, which was later identified as garlic, because in Norway at that time not many people used to eat.

That is, till now the police found the suitcase of that woman, a notepad written in a quote and a shop selling a pair of shoes near that woman and the smell of the woman was detected from the shop. Means the police have got four clues so far, but there was not a single clue that could give the address of the woman.

Now what the police came to know confused him even more because when the police searched all the hotels in Norway with the help of his scent, he came to know about the seven hotels where she had stayed. And where garlic was used in food.

PUZZLE IN PASSPORT

It was found that the identity of any hotel she used to check in was changed. Because in those days it was necessary to give passport while staying in any hotel, so her seven different passports baffled the police.

Now, on the basis of the text of the code word written on that notepad, and from the fingerprints of the anonymous woman found in seven hotels, it had come to know that she stayed in about nine hotels. And each time both her identity and name were different.

- Viking Hotel, Oslo where she stayed from 21 to 24 March 1970 under the name of Genevieve Lansier after coming from Louvain (Belgium).
- Hotel Bristol, Bergen, from Brussels (Belgium) and stayed under the name of Claudia Tilt from 24 to 25 March.
- Hotel Skandia, Bergen, from Brussels (Belgium) from March 25 to April 1, staying under the name of Claudia Tilt.
- KNA- Hotelet, Stavanger, here she stayed under the name of Claudia Nielsen from Ghent (Belgium) till 29 – 30 October.
- Neptun Hotel, Bergen, stayed here from 30 October to 5 November under the name of Alexia Zarne Marches, coming from Ljubljana (Slovenia).

Hotel Hordaheimen, Bergen, where she stayed from 19–23 November, coming from Ostend (Belgium) under the name of Elisabeth Leanhoffre

MURDER HIDDEN IN FOUR CLUES AND FOUR THEORIES

It took three months for the Norwegian police to extract so much complete information. And despite so much information, the police could not find any such identification of her, so that they could be ready to investigate the case further. The Norwegian police, who were reaching the same zero by roaming around were now completely frustrated. And he could not understand that who was going to die.

Till now the police had four clues and in the light of those clues, the police had made four theories. Out of those four theories, one theory was that there might be a spy who died, while the second theory was that she was an associate of a spy, in the third theory, the police found that woman as a courier working for a spy. But they were weaving the web of investigation while the fourth theory said that she could be a spy of a neighboring country who was killed by her enemies.

DEEP SECRET OF FOUR LANGUAGES

By now, the police had also come to know that the woman must have been speaking at least four languages, including French, Spanish, German and English.

With four clues, four languages and four theories trying to solve this five-decade-old mystery, Norwegian police turned to Interpol for help when they were exhausted. After gathering dust in the files for five decades, the case had once again come to the table of investigation.

In 2016, Norwegian investigators, with the help of Interpol, set a new task to trace the DNA of this woman from anywhere in the world. That is, now with the newly developed technology, the police around the world together did not want to let this 52 year old mystery remain a mystery anymore. But it will be interesting to see when the knot of this mystery opens.

SUICIDAL NOTE

A 25-year-old boy committed suicide in Delhi's Budh Vihar area, but before killing himself, he killed his mother and stayed in the same house with his mother's dead body for four whole days. He wrote a suicide note of 77 pages. This suicide note was written in the South Indian language, Kannada.

What was in this suicide note?

The boy's name was Kshitij. His mother's name was Mithilesh. This incident happened on September 1, but Kshitij had killed his mother three days earlier.

When her friend called on her mother's phone, the secret was revealed...

Actually, Mithilesh's friend called him on the day of the incident. Kshitij picked up the phone. He asked why his mother's phone was not being picked up. Then Kshitij had blown their senses by saying that he had killed his mother and now he was going to kill himself. Mithilesh's friend was shocked to hear this. He immediately called the police and told the whole thing. When the police team reached home at eight o'clock on Sunday night, all the doors of the house were locked. As soon as the police entered inside from the balcony of the house, they found the dead bodies of mother and son. The body of the mother was in the bathroom while Kshitij was lying dead in the room. His throat was also slit and blood was splattered all over.

A diary, the story of two deaths in the last 77 pages of the diary...

Police found a diary near Kshitij's dead body. The reason for two deaths were written in the last 77 pages of this diary. In a 77-page suicide note, Kshitij wrote that he was a victim of depression. According to the suicide note, he had strangled his mother to death with a wire and later slit her throat with a cutter. Kshitij wrote in the suicide note that he freed his ailing mother from her illness. He stayed with his mother's dead body for two days. He poured Ganges water on his mother's body and also recited Bhagwat Katha. He also sprayed deo continuously in the house to remove the stench when the dead body was decomposing.

According to the suicide note written by Kshitij, he had no friends. After the death of his father, the financial condition of the house had become very bad. Along with this, the mother was also often ill. He was also not keeping well for some time. There was no money for treatment.

He was told that he was brought up well. His father had a government job. He taught him in a reputed school. Later, they started ignoring. He was the most timid, submissive kid in the class. He had only two friends in the name of friend. who used to make fun of him. He complained to the teacher many times, but no one would listen. While getting on and off the school bus, he used to have a strange feeling of fear, shame, nervousness. His mother was his hope. After father's departure, mother and he were left alone. Her father left her at a time when she needed him the most.

While telling about his mother, Kshitij further wrote that for his good upbringing, the mother also sewed. His mother used to say that he should start teaching tuition to some small children. He was horrified to hear. When he was in tenth, his father died. He was born after 14 years of his parents. He was their only son and took admission in SOL of Delhi University but luck cheated. He failed twice. Depression persisted. He had been awake for five nights. He couldn't sleep. Sometimes he remained unconscious. Diseases were being filled inside him.

Referring to mother and father, Kshitij wrote at one place that his mother used to interrupt him many times. She was troubled by high BP. His father was very brave. His mother used to tell that when he was small, father took him in his arms and went to the hospital. There the monkeys wanted to drag him away from his lap but his father held him tight and chased away those monkeys.

THOSE LAST FOUR DAYS...

THURSDAY

From Thursday he started writing this suicide note and on Sunday he committed suicide. On Thursday, first he killed his mother. Kshitij had written in his suicide that he wanted to die for the last two years, wanted to free his mother from sorrow before dying. Mother used to go to satsang every Sunday. Last time also when mother came from there, there was a little argument and a little laughter too. There was cobweb in mother's eyes, it seems she had cataract. Now he wanted to die. Today was Thursday. He had used the cable of the bike to strangle his mother so that the mother did not feel pain due to death.

Further he wrote that as soon as he tightened the wire the mother fainted and fell down in 4 to 5 seconds. He knew that if oxygen did not reach the brain, death occurred. As soon as the mother fell, he kept her head in his lap. Kept her throat choked for eight to ten minutes. He was crying by pressing his mouth. All Thursday he had been crying day and night. He was missing his father a lot. Mother's eyes were open even after death. She tried to stop, but could not.

FRIDAY

Mother's face washed with Gangajal

He writes that today is Friday. The dead body of the mother is not being seen. He has washed his mother's face with the water of the Ganges. Sitting near him, reading the 18th chapter of the Bhagavad Gita. He could not read the entire Bhagavad Gita. He has kept the Bhagavad Gita on his mother's chest. Now it was his turn to commit suicide. First he tried to buy a pistol. Then came the idea of the electric cutter. He went to the market. Asked for electric cutter from two shopkeepers. Both did not give. Don't know why they started asking him strange questions. He returned home at night and cried a lot sitting near the dead body of his mother. What would have happened if there was a father?

THIRD DAY SATURDAY

Kshitij writes that it has been 71 hours since mother's death. It'd starting to stink. Mother's neck had been cut with a cutter. The smell started coming from Friday evening. He dragged the dead body of the mother and took it to the bathroom. The door was closed so that the smell does not come. He just wanted to complete the suicide note. The stench had spread in the house. today was Saturday. He has a empty stomach for three days. Haven't eaten anything. He remembered that he had kept hot water in the kitchen to drink.

WEARING A MASK KEPT WRITING SUICIDE NOTE (SUNDAY)

He was writing everything in the suicide note. He further wrote that the smell in the room was not stopping. Due to this, his health has also started deteriorating. He has burnt the wooden pencil shavings. Incense had been lit. A nutmeg was kept in the house, that too had been burnt. All the deo had also been sprinkled. He would complete the suicide note by wearing a mask. Today was Sunday. It was now two o'clock in the afternoon. Till now, since three days, the property dealer had come three times with the tenants to show the floor on rent, but today he would complete the note in any case.

He kept writing for a long time on Sunday because he wanted to complete the suicide note. He had further written that today is Sunday, mother has to go to satsang. Mother's friend is calling again and again. First on mother's phone, now my phone is ringing. He picked up the phone. Mother's friend is asking, Mithilesh is not picking up the phone, where is she? He said that the mother is dead, he killed her four days ago, now he is preparing to die. It is very scary to see all this. Mother's brother-in-law took care of him like a father after his father left, so he declares that his bike will be in his name after he dies. His wish is that his mother's last rites should be performed by his aunt.

THE JUDGE'S HOUSE

It was April and John Moore was studying for an important examination. As the date of the exam came nearer, he decided to go somewhere and read by himself. He did not want the amusements of the seaside, or the beauties of the countryside. He decided to find a quiet, ordinary little town and work there undisturbed. He packed his suitcases with clothes and books. Then he looked in a railway timetable for a town that he did not know. He found one, and bought a ticket to go there. He did not tell anyone where he was going. After all, he did not want to be disturbed.

That is how Moore arrived at Benchurch. It was a market town, and once a week it was quite busy for a few hours. The rest of the time it was a very quiet, sleepy little place. Moore spent his first night at the only hotel in the town. The landlady was very kind and helpful, but the hotel was not really quiet enough for him. The second day he started looking for a house to rent.

There was only one place that he liked. It was more than quiet – it was deserted and very lonely. It was a big, old seventeenth-century house. It had tiny windows like a prison, and a high brick wall all round it. It would be hard to imagine a more unwelcoming place. But it suited Moore perfectly. He went to find the local lawyer, who was responsible for the house.

Mr Carnford, the lawyer, was very happy to rent the house to him.

'I'd be glad to let you have it free,' he said, 'just to have somebody living in it again after all these years. It's been empty so long that people have spread a lot of foolish stories about it. You'll be able to prove that the stories are wrong.'

Moore did not think it was necessary to ask the lawyer for more details of the 'foolish stories'. He paid his rent, and Mr Carnford gave him the name of an old servant to look after him. He came away from the lawyer's office with the keys of the house in his pocket. He then went to Mrs Wood, the landlady of the hotel.

`I'm renting a house for a few weeks,' he said. `Can you advise me about shopping, please? What do you think I shall need?'

`Where are you going to stay, sir?' the landlady asked. Moore told her.

She threw up her hands in horror. `Not the Judge's House!' she said, and she grew pale as she spoke. He asked her to tell him more about the house. `Why is it called the Judge's House?' he said, `and why doesn't anyone want to live in it?

'`Well, sir,' she said, `a long time ago – no, I don't know how long – a judge lived there. He was a hard, cruel judge, sir – a real hanging judge. He showed no mercy to anyone. But as for the house itself – well, I can't say. I've often asked, but nobody could tell me for certain.' She found it hard to explain. The general feeling in the town was that there was something strange about the Judge's House. `As for me, sir,' she said, `I won't stay there alone, not for all the money in the bank!'

Then she apologized to Moore. `I'm sorry to worry you, sir, really I am. But if you were my son I wouldn't let you stay there one night on your own. I'd go there myself and pull the big alarm bell that's Ghost Stories 2 7 on the roof!'

Moore was grateful for her kindness and her anxiety. `How good of you to be so anxious about me, Mrs Wood!' he said. But there's really no need to worry. I'm studying for an important examination and I have no time for horrors or mysteries.'

The landlady kindly promised to do his shopping for him. Moore then went to see the old servant whom Mr Carnford had recommended to him. Her name was Mrs Dempster, and she seemed pleasant and eager to please her new master.

When he returned with her to the Judge's House two hours later, he found Mrs Wood waiting outside it. She had several people with her – men and boys carrying parcels, and another two men with a bed. `

But there are beds in the house!' cried Moore in surprise. `And nobody's slept in them for fifty years or more! No, sir, I won't let you risk your life in an old, damp bed.'

The landlady was obviously curious to see the inside of the house. At the same time she was clearly afraid. At the smallest noise she held nervously to Moore's arm. Together they explored the whole house. After his exploration, Moore decided to live in the dining-room. It was big enough for both working and sleeping. Mrs Wood and Mrs Dempster began to arrange everything. Soon the baskets were unpacked. Moore saw that kind Mrs Wood had brought many good things from her own kitchen. Before she left she turned to Moore and said, `I do hope you will be all right, sir. But I must say – I couldn't sleep here, with all those ghosts!'

When she left, Mrs Dempster laughed. `Ghosts!' she said. `Ghosts! There are no ghosts! There are rats and insects, and doors that need oiling. There are windows that blow open in the wind. . . Look at the old oak walls of this room, sir. They are old – hundreds of years old! Don't you think there'll be rats and insects behind the wood? You'll see plenty of rats here, sir, but you won't see any ghosts – I'm sure of that. Now you go and have a nice walk, sir. And when you come back, I'll have this room all ready for you.'

She kept her promise. When Moore returned he found the room clean and neat. A fire was burning in the ancient fireplace. She had lit the lamp and put his supper ready on the table.

`Good night, sir,' she said. `I have to go now and get my husband's supper. I'll see you in the morning.'

`This is wonderful!' said Moore to himself as he ate Mrs Dempster's excellent food. When he had finished his supper, he pushed the dishes to the other end of the table. He put more wood on the fire and began to study.

Moore worked without stopping until about eleven o'clock. Then he put some more wood on the fire. He also made a pot of tea. He was enjoying himself very much. The fire was burning brightly. The firelight danced on the old oak walls and threw strange shadows around the room. His tea tasted excellent, and there was nobody to disturb him. Then for the first time he noticed how much noise the rats were making.

`Were they making all this noise while I was studying?' he thought. `No, I don't think they were. Perhaps they were afraid of me at first. Now they have become braver, and they are running about as usual.

' How busy they were! And what a lot of noise they made! Up and down they rushed, behind the old oak walls, over the ceiling and under the floor. Moore remembered Mrs Dempster's words: `You'll see plenty of rats, but you won't see any ghosts.' `Well,' he said with a smile, `she was right about the rats, anyway!'

He picked up the lamp and looked around the room. `How strange,' he said to himself. `Why doesn't anybody want to live in this beautiful old house?' The oak walls were very beautiful. There were some old pictures on the walls, but they were covered with dust and dirt and he could not see them clearly. Here and there he saw small holes in the walls. From time to time the curious face of a rat stared at him. Then with a scratch and a squeak, it was gone.

The thing that interested him most, however, was the rope of the great alarm bell on the roof. The rope hung down in a corner of the room on the right-hand side of the fireplace. He found a huge, high-backed oak chair and pulled it up beside the fire. There he sat and drank his last cup of tea. Then he put more wood on the fire and sat down at the table again with his books. For a time the rats disturbed him with their scratching and squeaking. But he got used to the noise, and soon he forgot everything except his work.

Suddenly he looked up. Something had disturbed him, but he did not know what it was. He sat up and listened. The room was silent. That was it! The noise of the rats had stopped. `That's what disturbed me!' said Moore with a smile. He looked around the room – and saw an enormous rat. It was sitting on the great high-backed chair by the fire, and it was staring at him with hate in its small red eyes. Moore picked up a book and pretended to throw it. But the rat did not move. It showed its great white teeth angrily, and its cruel eyes shone mercilessly in the lamplight.

`Why, you –' cried Moore. He picked up the poker from the fireplace and jumped up. Before he could hit the rat, however, it jumped to the floor with a squeak. It ran up the rope of the alarm bell and disappeared in the darkness. Strangely, the squeaks and scratches of the rats in the walls began again. By this time Moore no longer felt like working. Outside the house the birds were singing: soon it would be morning. He climbed into bed and immediately fell asleep.

He slept so deeply that he did not hear Mrs Dempster come in. She dusted the room and made his breakfast. Then she woke him with a cup of tea.

After breakfast he put a book in his pocket and went out for a walk. On the way he bought a few sandwiches. (`Then I shan't have to stop for lunch,' he said to himself). He found a pretty, quiet little park and spent most of the day there, studying. On his way home he called at the hotel to thank Mrs Wood for her kindness. She looked at him searchingly.

`You must not work too hard, sir. You look pale this morning. Too much studying isn't good for anyone. But tell me, sir, did you have a good night? Mrs Dempster told me you were still asleep when she went in.'

`Oh, I was all right,' said Moore with a smile. `The ghosts haven't troubled me yet. But the rats had a party last night! There was one old devil with red eyes. He sat up on the chair by the fire. He didn't move until I picked up the poker. Then he ran up the rope of the alarm bell. I didn't see where he went. It was too dark.'

`Dear God!' cried Mrs Wood, `an old devil sitting by the fire! Take care, sir, take care.'

`What do you mean?' asked Moore in surprise.

`An old devil! The old devil, perhaps.' Moore started to laugh.

`Please forgive me, Mrs Wood,' he said at last. `I just couldn't help laughing at the idea of the Devil himself sitting by my fire . . . ' And he began to laugh again. Then he went home for dinner. That evening the noise of the rats began earlier. After dinner he sat down beside the fire and drank his tea. Then he sat down at the table and started to work again.

The rats disturbed him more than the previous night. They scratched and squeaked and ran about, and stared at him from the holes in the walls. Their eyes shone like tiny lamps in the firelight. But Moore was becoming used to them. They seemed playful rather than aggressive. Sometimes the bravest rats ran out onto the floor or across the tops of the pictures. Now and again, when they disturbed him, Moore shook his papers at them. They ran to their holes at once. And so the early part of the night passed quite quietly.

Moore worked hard for several hours.

All at once he was disturbed by a sudden silence. There was not a sound of running, or scratching, or squeaking. The huge room was as silent as the grave. Moore remembered the previous night. He looked at the chair by the fireside – and got a terrible shock. There, on the great high-backed oak chair, sat the same enormous rat. It was staring at him with hate.

Without thinking, Moore picked up the nearest book and threw it. It missed, and the rat did not move. So Moore again picked up the poker. Again the rat ran up the rope of the alarm bell. And once more the other rats started their scratching and squeaking. Moore was unable to see where the rat had gone. The light of the lamp did not reach as far as the high ceiling, and the fire had burned low. Moore looked at his watch. It was almost midnight. He put more wood on the fire and made a pot of tea. Then he sat down in the great oak chair by the fire and enjoyed his tea.

`I wonder where that old rat went just now,' he thought. `I must buy a rat trap in the morning.' He lit another lamp. He placed it so that it would shine into the right-hand corner of the wall by the fireplace. He got several books ready to throw at the creature. Finally he lifted the rope of the alarm bell. He put it on the table and fixed the end of it under the lamp.

As he handled the rope, Moore noticed how pliable it was. `You could hang a man with it,' he thought. Then he stood back and admired his preparations.

`There, my friend,' he said aloud, `I think I'll learn your secret this time!'

He started work again, and was soon lost in his studies. But once again he was disturbed by a sudden silence. Then the bell rope moved a little, and the lamp on top of the rope moved too. Moore made sure that his books were ready for throwing. Then he looked along the rope. As he looked, the great rat dropped from the rope onto the old oak chair. It sat there staring at him angrily. He picked up a book and aimed it at the rat. The creature jumped cleverly to one side. Moore threw another book, but without success. Then, as Moore stood with a third book in his hand, ready to throw, the rat squeaked and seemed to be afraid. Moore threw the book and it hit the rat's side. With a squeak of pain and fear, and a look of real hate, it ran up the back of the chair and made a great jump onto the rope of the alarm bell. It ran up the rope like lightning, while the heavy lamp shook with its desperate speed. Moore watched the rat carefully. By the light of the second lamp, he saw it disappear through a hole in one of the great pictures on the wall.

`I shall check my unpleasant little visitor's home in the morning,' said Moore to himself as he picked up his books from the floor. `The third picture from the fireplace: I shan't forget.' He examined the books. He picked up the third book that he had thrown. `This is the one that hurt him!' he said to himself. Then his face turned pale. `Why – it's my mother's old Bible! How strange!' He sat down to work again, and once more the rats in the walls started their noise. This did not worry him. Compared with the huge rat, these ones seemed almost friendly. But he could not work. At last he closed his books and went to bed. The first red light of morning was shining through the window as he closed his eyes.

He slept heavily but uneasily, and he had unpleasant dreams. Then Mrs Dempster woke him as usual with a cup of tea, and he felt better. But his first request to her surprised the old servant very much. `Mrs Dempster, while I'm out today, will you please dust or wash those pictures – particularly the third one from the fireplace. I want to see what they are.'

Again Moore spent most of the day studying happily in the park. On his way home he again visited Mrs Wood at the hotel. She had a visitor with her in her comfortable sitting-room.

`Sir,' said the landlady, `this is Doctor Thornhill.' As soon as she had introduced them, the doctor began to ask Moore a great many questions. `I'm sure,' said Moore to himself, `that the good doctor did not call here by accident.' He turned to Doctor Thornhill.

`Doctor, I'll gladly answer all your questions, if you'll just answer one of mine.'

The doctor seemed surprised, but he agreed at once.

`Did Mrs Wood ask you to come here and advise me?' asked Moore. The doctor looked surprised. Mrs Wood's face turned very red and she looked away. But the doctor was an honest, friendly man, and he answered quickly, `She did, but she didn't want you to know. She's worried about you. She, doesn't like you staying there all alone, and she thinks you study too hard and drink too much strong tea. She asked me to give you some good advice. I was once a student too, you know, so I know what I'm talking about.'

Moore smiled and held out his hand to Doctor Thornhill. `I must thank you for your kindness – and you too, Mrs Wood. I promise to take no more strong tea, and I'll be in bed by one o'clock. There, will that please you both?'

`Very much,' said Doctor Thornhill. `Now tell us all about that old house.'

Moore told them all about the events of the previous nights. When he told them how he had thrown the Bible, Mrs Wood gave a little scream. When Moore had finished his story, Doctor Thornhill looked very serious.

`The rat always ran up the rope of the alarm bell?' he asked. `Always.'

`I suppose you know,' said the doctor, `what the rope is?'

`No, I don't,' said Moore

`It is the hangman's rope,' said the doctor. `After the judge condemned someone to death, the unfortunate man was hanged with that rope.' Mrs Wood gave another scream. The doctor went to fetch her a glass of water.

When he returned, he looked hard at Moore. `Listen, young man,' he said. `If anything happens to you tonight, don't hesitate to ring the alarm bell. I shall be working quite late tonight too, and I'll keep my ears open. Now don't forget!

' Moore laughed. `I'm sure I shan't need to do that!' he said, and went home for his dinner.

`I don't like that young man's story,' said Doctor Thornhill after Moore had left. `Perhaps he imagined most of it. All the same, I'll listen tonight for the alarm bell. Perhaps we'll reach him in time to help him.'

When Moore arrived home, Mrs Dempster had already left. But his supper was ready for him. The lamp was burning brightly and there was a good fire in the fireplace. It was a cold, windy evening, but the room was warm and inviting. For a few minutes after he came in, the rats were quiet. But, as before, they soon became used to his presence in the room. Soon they started their noise again. He was glad to hear them. He remembered how silent they had been when the great rat appeared. Moore soon forgot the squeaking and scratching. He sat down to his dinner with a light heart. After dinner he opened his books, determined to get some work done. For an hour or two he worked very well. Then his concentration weakened, and he looked up. It was a stormy night. The whole house seemed to shake, and the wind whistled down the chimneys with a strange, unnatural sound. The force of the wind shook the alarm bell. The pliable rope rose and fell a Ghost Stories 6 11 little, and the bottom of it hit the oak floor with a hard and hollow sound. As Moore watched it, he remembered the doctor's words: `It's the hangman's rope.' He went over to the corner by the fireplace and took the rope in his hand. He looked at it very hard. He wondered how many people had died on the end of that rope. As he held it, the movement of the bell on the roof still lifted it now and again. Then he felt a new movement. The rope seemed to tremble, as if something was moving along it. At the same time, the noise of the rats stopped. Moore looked up, and saw the great rat coming down towards him. It was staring at him with hate. Moore dropped the rope and jumped back with a cry. The rat turned, ran up the rope again and disappeared. At the same moment Moore realized that the noise of the other rats had begun again. `Very well, my friend,' thought Moore, `let's investigate your hiding place.' He lit the other lamp. He remembered that the rat had disappeared inside the third picture on the right. He picked up the lamp and carried it across to the picture. He almost dropped the lamp. He stepped back at once, and the sweat of fear was upon his pale face. His knees shook. His whole body trembled like a leaf. But he was young and brave, and he moved forward again with his lamp. Mrs Dempster had dusted and washed the picture, and Moore could now see it quite clearly. It showed a judge. He had a cruel, clever, merciless face, with a big curved nose and very bright, hard eyes. As Moore looked into those eyes, he realized that he had seen that look before. The great rat's eyes were exactly the same. They held the same look of hate and cruelty. Then the noise of the rats stopped again, and Moore became conscious of another pair of eyes looking at him. The great rat was staring at him from the hole in the corner of the picture. But Moore took no notice of the creature and continued to examine the picture. The Judge was sitting in a great, high-backed oak chair, on the right-hand side of a great stone fireplace. In the corner a rope hung down from the ceiling. With a feeling of horror, Moore recognized the room where he now stood. He looked around him, as if he expected to see another presence there. Then he looked across to the corner of the fireplace. He froze with fear and the lamp fell from his trembling hand. There, in the Judge's chair, sat the rat. The rope hung behind, exactly as it did in the picture. The rat looked at Moore with the same merciless stare as the Judge in the picture. But there was a new, triumphant look in the small red eyes. Everything was silent except for the storm outside. `The lamp!' thought Moore desperately. Fortunately it was a metal one, and the oil had not caught fire. However, he had to put it out. In doing so, he forgot his fears for a moment. Then he stopped and thought. `I can't go on like this,' he said to himself. `The doctor is right. Late hours and strong tea are not good for me. They just make me nervous. However, I'm all right now.' He made himself a warm, milky drink and sat down to work. Nearly an hour later a sudden silence disturbed him again. Outside, the storm was growling and whistling as loudly as ever. The rain drummed on the windows. But inside the house everything was as quiet as the grave. Moore listened carefully, and then he heard a strange squeaking noise. It came from the corner of the room where the rope hung down. At first he thought the rope itself was making the sound. Then he looked up and saw the great rat. It was chewing the rope with its ugly yellow teeth. It had almost bitten through it, and, as Moore watched, part of the rope fell to the floor. Only a short piece was still attached to the bell, and the rat was still hanging onto it. Now the rope began to swing backwards and forwards. Moore felt a moment of terrible fear. `Now I can never ring the alarm bell,' he thought. Then he was filled with anger. He picked up the book he was reading, and threw it violently at the rat. He aimed it well. But before the book could hit the creature, it dropped off the rope and landed on the floor. At once Moore rushed towards it, but the rat ran away and disappeared into the shadows. `Let's have another rat hunt before bed!' said Moore to himself. He picked up the lamp – and almost dropped it again. The figure of the Judge had disappeared from the picture. The chair and the details of the room were still there. But the man himself had gone. Frozen with horror, Moore moved slowly round. He began to shake and tremble. His strength left him, and he was unable to move a muscle. He could only Ghost Stories 6 12 see and hear. There, on the great high–backed oak chair sat the Judge. His merciless eyes stared at Moore. There was a smile of triumph on his cruel mouth. Slowly he lifted up a black hat. Moore's heart was drumming wildly. There was a strange singing noise in his ears. Outside, the wind was as wild as ever. Then, above the screams of the wind, he heard the great clock striking in the market place. He stood and listened, stiff and unmoving. The triumph on the Judge's face grew. As the clock struck twelve, the Judge placed the black hat on his head. Slowly and deliberately, he rose from his chair and picked up the piece of rope from the floor. He pulled it through his hands. Slowly and carefully he made the thick, pliable rope into a noose. He tested the noose with his foot. He pulled hard at it until he was pleased with it. Then he began to move slowly and carefully past the table, on the opposite side to Moore. Then with one quick movement he stood in front of the door. Moore was trapped! All this time, the Judge's eyes never left Moore's.

Moore stared into the cruel eyes, like a bird watching a cat. He saw the Judge coming nearer with his noose. He saw him throw the noose towards him. Desperately Moore threw himself to one side, and saw the rope fall harmlessly to the floor. Again the Judge raised the noose and tried to catch Moore. Again and again he tried. And all the time he stared mercilessly at the student. `He's just playing with me,' thought Moore, `like a cat playing with a bird. Soon he'll catch me, and hang me . . . ' He looked desperately behind him. Hundreds of rats were watching him with bright, anxious little eyes. Then he saw that the rope of the alarm bell was covered with rats. As he watched, more and more were pouring down onto the rope, from the round hole in the ceiling that led to the bell itself. The rats were hanging from the rope, and there were so many of them that the rope was swinging backwards and forwards. The alarm bell began to ring, softly at first, then more strongly. At the sound, the Judge looked up. A devilish anger spread across his face. His eyes burned like red jewels. Outside there was a sudden, deafening crash of thunder. The Judge raised his noose again, while the rats ran desperately up and down the rope of the alarm bell. This time, instead of throwing the rope, the Judge moved nearer to Moore, and held the noose open. Moore was unable to move. He stood there like a stone figure. He felt the Judge's icy fingers and the pliable rope against his neck. He felt the noose against his throat. Then the Judge picked up the stiff body of the student in his arms. He carried him over to the great oak chair and stood him on it. Then, stepping up beside him, the Judge put up his hand and caught the rope of the alarm bell. At his touch the rats ran away, squeaking with fear. They disappeared through the hole in the ceiling. Then the Judge took the end of the noose which was around Moore's neck. He tied it to the hanging bell rope. Then he climbed down, and pulled away the chair.

When the alarm bell of the Judge's House began to ring, a crowd soon gathered. People came running with lanterns and torches, and soon hundreds of people were hurrying to the house. They knocked loudly at the door, but there was no reply. Then they broke down the door, and poured into the Ghost Stories 8 13 great dining-room. The Doctor was the first to reach Moore. But it was too late. There at the end of the bell rope hung the body of the student. The Judge stared out once more from his picture. But on his face there was a smile of triumph.

THE INVISIBLE MAN

In the cool blue twilight of two steep streets in Camden Town, the shop at the corner, a confectioner's, glowed like the butt of a cigar. One should rather say, perhaps, like the butt of a firework, for the light was of many colours and some complexity, broken up by many mirrors and dancing on many gilt and gaily-coloured cakes and sweetmeats. Against this one fiery glass were glued the noses of many gutter-snipes, for the chocolates were all wrapped in those red and gold and green metallic colours which are almost better than chocolate itself; and the huge white wedding-cake in the window was somehow at once remote and satisfying, just as if the whole North Pole were good to eat. Such rainbow provocations could naturally collect the youth of the neighbourhood up to the ages of ten or twelve. But this corner was also attractive to youth at a later stage; and a young man, not less than twenty-four, was staring into the same shop window. To him, also, the shop was of fiery charm, but this attraction was not wholly to be explained by chocolates; which, however, he was far from despising.

He was a tall, burly, red-haired young man, with a resolute face but a listless manner. He carried under his arm a flat, grey portfolio of black-and-white sketches, which he had sold with more or less success to publishers ever since his uncle (who was an admiral) had disinherited him for socialism, because of a lecture which he had delivered against that economic theory. His name was John Turnbull Angus.

Entering at last, he walked through the confectioner's shop to the back room, which was a sort of pastry-cook restaurant, merely raising his hat to the young lady who was serving there. She was a dark, elegant, alert girl in black, with a high colour and very quick, dark eyes; and after the ordinary interval she followed him into the inner room to take his order.

His order was evidently a usual one. "I want, please," he said with precision, "one half penny bun and a small cup of black coffee." Before the girl could turn away he added, "Also, I want you to marry me."

The young lady of the shop stiffened suddenly and said, "Those are jokes I don't allow."

The red-haired young man lifted his grey eyes of an unexpected gravity.

"Really and truly," he said, "it's as serious — as serious as the half penny bun. It is expensive, like the bun; one pays for it. It is indigestible, like the bun. It hurts."

The dark young lady had never taken her dark eyes off him, but seemed to be studying him with almost tragic exactitude. At the end of her scrutiny she had something like the shadow of a smile, and she sat down in a chair.

"Don't you think," observed Angus, absently, "that it's rather cruel to eat these half penny buns? They might grow up into penny buns. I shall give up these brutal sports when we are married."

The dark young lady rose from her chair and walked to the window, evidently in a state of strong but not unsympathetic cogitation. When at last she swung round again with an air of resolution she was bewildered to observe that the young man was carefully laying out on the table various objects from the shop-window. They included a pyramid of highly coloured sweets, several plates of sandwiches, and the two decanters containing that mysterious port and sherry which are peculiar to pastry-cooks. In the middle of this neat arrangement he had carefully let down the enormous load of white sugared cake which had been the huge ornament of the window.

"What on earth are you doing?" she asked.

"Duty, my dear Laura," he began.

"Oh, for Lord's sake, stop a minute," she cried, "and don't talk to me in that way. I mean, what is all that?"

"A ceremonial meal, Miss Hope."

"And what is that?" she asked impatiently, pointing to the mountain of sugar.

"The wedding-cake, Mrs. Angus," he said.

The girl marched to that article, removed it with some clatter, and put it back in the shop window; she then returned, and, putting her elegant elbows on the table, regarded the young man not unfavourably but with considerable exasperation.

"You don't give me any time to think," she said.

"I'm not such a fool," he answered; "that's my Christian humility."

She was still looking at him; but she had grown considerably graver behind the smile.

"Mr. Angus," she said steadily, "before there is a minute more of this nonsense I must tell you something about myself as shortly as I can.'"

"Delighted," replied Angus gravely. "You might tell me something about myself, too, while you are about it."

"Oh, do hold your tongue and listen," she said. "It's nothing that I'm ashamed of, and it isn't even anything that I'm specially sorry about. But what would you say if there were something that is no business of mine and yet is my nightmare?"

"In that case," said the man seriously, "I should suggest that you bring back the cake."

"Well, you must listen to the story first," said Laura, persistently. "To begin with, I must tell you that my father owned the inn called the 'Red Fish' at Ludbury, and I used to serve people in the bar."

"I have often wondered," he said, "why there was a kind of a Christian air about this one confectioner's shop."

"Ludbury is a sleepy, grassy little hole in the Eastern Counties, and the only kind of people who ever came to the 'Red Fish' were occasional commercial travellers, and for the rest, the most awful people you can see, only you've never seen them. I mean little, loungy men, who had just enough to live on and had nothing to do but lean about in bar-rooms and bet on horses, in bad clothes that were just too good for them. Even these wretched young rotters were not very common at our house; but there were two of them that were a lot too common — common in every sort of way. They both lived on money of their own, and were wearisomely idle and over-dressed. But yet, I was a bit sorry for them, because I half believe they slunk into our little empty bar because each of them had a slight deformity; the sort of thing that some yokels laugh at. It wasn't exactly a deformity either; it was more an oddity. One of them was a surprisingly small man, something like a dwarf, or at least like a jockey. He was not at all jockeyish to look at, though; he had a round black head and a well-trimmed black beard, bright eyes like a bird's; he jingled money in his pockets; he jangled a great gold watch chain; and he never turned up except dressed just too much like a gentleman to be one. He was no fool though, though a futile idler; he was curiously clever at all kinds of things that couldn't be the slightest use; a sort of impromptu conjuring; making fifteen matches set fire to each other like a regular firework; or cutting a banana or some such thing into a dancing doll. His name was Isidore Smythe; and I can see him still, with his little dark face, just coming up to the counter, making a jumping kangaroo out of five cigars."

"The other fellow was more silent and more ordinary; but somehow he alarmed me much more than poor little Smythe. He was very tall and slight, and light-haired; his nose had a high bridge, and he might almost have been handsome in a spectral sort of way; but he had one of the most appalling squints I have ever seen or heard of. When he looked straight at you, you didn't know where you were yourself, let alone what he was looking at. I fancy this sort of disfigurement embittered the poor chap a little; for while Smythe was ready to show off his monkey tricks anywhere, James Welkin (that was the squinting man's name) never did anything except soak in our bar parlour, and go for great walks by himself in the flat, grey country all round. All the same, I think Smythe, too, was a little sensitive about being so small, though he carried it off more smartly. And so it was that I was really puzzled, as well as startled, and very sorry, when they both offered to marry me in the same week."

"Well, I did what I've since thought was perhaps a silly thing. But, after all, these freaks were my friends in a way; and I had a horror of their thinking. I refused them for the real reason, which was that they were so impossibly ugly. So I made up some gas of another sort, about never meaning to marry anyone who hadn't carved his way in the world. I said it was a point of principle with me not to live on money that was just inherited like theirs. Two days after I had talked in this well-meaning sort of way, the whole trouble began. The first thing I heard was that both of them had gone off to seek their fortunes, as if they were in some silly fairy tale."

"Well, I've never seen either of them from that day to this. But I've had two letters from the little man called Smythe, and really they were rather exciting."

"Ever heard of the other man?" asked Angus.

"No, he never wrote," said the girl, after an instant's hesitation. "Smythe's first letter was simply to say that he had started out walking with Welkin to London; but Welkin was such a good walker that the little man dropped out of it, and took a rest by the roadside. He happened to be picked up by some travelling show, and, partly because he was nearly a dwarf, and partly because he was really a clever little wretch, he got on quite well in the show business, and was soon sent up to the Aquarium, to do some tricks that I forget. That was his first letter. His second was much more of a startler, and I only got it last week."

The man called Angus emptied his coffee-cup and regarded her with mild and patient eyes. Her own mouth took a slight twist of laughter as she resumed, "I suppose you've seen on the hoardings all about this 'Smythe's Silent Service'? Or you must be the only person that hasn't. Oh, I don't know much about it, it's some clockwork invention for doing all the housework by machinery. You know the sort of thing: 'Press a Button — A Butler who Never Drinks.' 'Turn a Handle — Ten Housemaids who Never Flirt.' You must have seen the advertisements. Well, whatever these machines are, they are making pots of money; and they are making it all for that little imp whom I knew down in Ludbury. I can't help feeling pleased the poor little chap has fallen on his feet; but the plain fact is, I'm in terror of his turning up any minute and telling me he's carved his way in the world — as he certainly has."

"And the other man?" repeated Angus with a sort of obstinate quietude.

Laura Hope got to her feet suddenly. "My friend," she said, "I think you are a witch. Yes, you are quite right. I have not seen a line of the other man's writing; and I have no more notion than the dead of what or where he is. But it is of him that I am frightened. It is he who is all about my path. It is he who has half driven me mad. Indeed, I think he has driven me mad; for I have felt him where he could not have been, and I have heard his voice when he could not have spoken."

"Well, my dear," said the young man, cheerfully, "if he were Satan himself, he is done for now you have told somebody. One goes mad all alone, old girl. But when was it you fancied you felt and heard our squinting friend?"

"I heard James Welkin laugh as plainly as I hear you speak," said the girl, steadily. "There was nobody there, for I stood just outside the shop at the corner, and could see down both streets at once. I had forgotten how he laughed, though his laugh was as odd as his squint. I had not thought of him for nearly a year. But it's a solemn truth that a few seconds later the first letter came from his rival."

"Did you ever make the spectre speak or squeak, or anything?" asked Angus, with some interest.

Laura suddenly shuddered, and then said, with an unshaken voice, "Yes. Just when I had finished reading the second letter from Isidore Smythe announcing his success. Just then, I heard Welkin say, 'He shan't have you, though.' It was quite plain, as if he were in the room. It is awful, I think I must be mad."

"If you really were mad," said the young man, "you would think you must be sane. But certainly there seems to me to be something a little rum about this unseen gentleman. Two heads are better than one — I spare you allusions to any other organs and really, if you would allow me, as a sturdy, practical man, to bring back the wedding-cake out of the window "

Even as he spoke, there was a sort of steely shriek in the street outside, and a small motor, driven at devilish speed, shot up to the door of the shop and stuck there. In the same flash of time a small man in a shiny top hat stood stamping in the outer room.

Angus, who had hitherto maintained hilarious ease from motives of mental hygiene, revealed the strain of his soul by striding abruptly out of the inner room and confronting the newcomer. A glance at him was quite sufficient to confirm the savage guesswork of a man in love. This very dapper but dwarfish figure, with the spike of black beard carried insolently forward, the clever un-restful eyes, the neat but very nervous fingers, could be none other than the man just described to him: Isidore Smythe, who made dolls out of banana skins and match-boxes; Isidore Smythe, who made millions out of undrinking butlers and unflirting housemaids of metal. For a moment the two men, instinctively understanding each other's air of possession, looked at each other with that curious cold generosity which is the soul of rivalry.

Mr. Smythe, however, made no allusion to the ultimate ground of their antagonism, but said simply and explosively, "Has Miss Hope seen that thing on the window?"

"On the window?" repeated the staring Angus.

"There's no time to explain other things," said the small millionaire shortly. "There's some tomfoolery going on here that has to be investigated."

He pointed his polished walking-stick at the window, recently depleted by the bridal preparations of Mr. Angus; and that gentleman was astonished to see along the front of the glass a long strip of paper pasted, which had certainly not been on the window when he looked through it some time before. Following the energetic Smythe outside into the street, he found that some yard and a half of stamp paper had been carefully gummed along the glass outside, and on this was written in straggly characters, "If you marry Smythe, he will die."

"Laura," said Angus, putting his big red head into the shop, "you're not mad."

"It's the writing of that fellow Welkin," said Smythe gruffly. "I haven't seen him for years, but he's always bothering me. Five times in the last fortnight he's had threatening letters left at my flat, and I can't even find out who leaves them, let alone if it is Welkin himself. The porter of the flats swears that no suspicious characters have been seen, and here he has pasted up a sort of dado on a public shop window, while the people in the shop — "

"Quite so," said Angus modestly, "while the people in the shop were having tea. Well, sir, I can assure you I appreciate your common sense in dealing so directly with the matter. We can talk about other things afterwards. The fellow cannot be very far off yet, for I swear there was no paper there when I went last to the window, ten or fifteen minutes ago. On the other hand, he's too far off to be chased, as we don't even know the direction. If you'll take my advice, Mr. Smythe, you'll put this at once in the hands of some energetic inquiry man, private rather than public. I know an extremely clever fellow, who has set up in business five minutes from here in your car. His name's Flambeau, and though his youth was a bit stormy, he's a strictly honest man now, and his brains are worth money. He lives in Lucknow Mansions, Hampstead."

"That is odd," said the little man, arching his black eyebrows. "I live, myself, in Himalaya Mansions, round the corner. Perhaps you might care to come with me; I can go to my rooms and sort out these queer Welkin documents, while you run round and get your friend the detective."

"You are very good," said Angus politely. "Well, the sooner we act the better."

Both men, with a queer kind of impromptu fairness, took the same sort of formal farewell of the lady, and both jumped into the brisk little car. As Smythe took the handles and they turned the great corner of the street, Angus was amused to see a gigantesque poster of "Smythe's Silent Service," with a picture of a huge headless iron doll, carrying a saucepan with the legend, "A Cook Who is Never Cross."

"I use them in my own flat," said the little black-bearded man, laughing, "partly for advertisements, and partly for real convenience. Honestly, and all above board, those big clockwork dolls of mine do bring your coals or claret or a timetable quicker than any live servants I've ever known, if you know which knob to press. But I'll never deny, between ourselves, that such servants have their disadvantages, too.

"Indeed?" said Angus; "is there something they can't do?"

"Yes," replied Smythe coolly; "they can't tell me who left those threatening letters at my flat."

The man's motor was small and swift like himself; in fact, like his domestic service, it was of his own invention. If he was an advertising quack, he was one who believed in his own wares. The sense of something tiny and flying was accentuated as they swept up long white curves of road in the dead but open daylight of evening. Soon the white curves came sharper and dizzier; they were upon ascending spirals, as they say in the modern religions. For, indeed, they were cresting a corner of London which is almost as precipitous as Edinburgh, if not quite so picturesque. Terrace rose above terrace, and the special tower of flats they sought, rose above them all to almost Egyptian height, gilt by the level sunset. The change, as they turned the corner and entered the crescent known as Himalayan Mansions, was as abrupt as the opening of a window; for they found that pile of flats sitting above London as above a green sea of slate. Opposite to the mansions, on the other side of the gravel crescent, was a bushy enclosure more like a steep hedge or dyke than a garden, and some way below that ran a strip of artificial water, a sort of canal, like the moat of that embowered fortress. As the car swept round the crescent it passed, at one corner, the stray stall of a man selling chestnuts; and right away at the other end of the curve, Angus could see a dim blue policeman walking slowly. These were the only human shapes in that high suburban solitude; but he had an irrational sense that they expressed the speechless poetry of London. He felt as if they were figures in a story.

The little car shot up to the right house like a bullet, and shot out its owner like a bomb shell. He was immediately inquiring of a tall commissionaire in shining braid, and a short porter in shirt sleeves, whether anybody or anything had been seeking his apartments. He was assured that nobody and nothing had passed these officials since his last inquiries; whereupon he and the slightly bewildered Angus were shot up in the lift like a rocket, till they reached the top floor.

"Just come in for a minute," said the breathless Smythe. "I want to show you those Welkin letters. Then you might run round the corner and fetch your friend." He pressed a button concealed in the wall, and the door opened of itself.

It opened on a long, commodious ante-room, of which the only arresting features, ordinarily speaking, were the rows of tall half-human mechanical figures that stood up on both sides like tailors' dummies. Like tailors' dummies they were headless; and like tailors' dummies they had a handsome unnecessary happiness in the shoulders, and a pigeon-breasted protuberance of chest; but barring this, they were not much more like a human figure than any automatic machine at a station that is about the human height. They had two great hooks like arms, for carrying trays; and they were painted pea-green, or vermilion, or black for convenience of distinction; in every other way they were only automatic machines and nobody would have looked twice at them. On this occasion, at least, nobody did. For between the two rows of these domestic dummies lay something more interesting than most of the mechanics of the world. It was a white, tattered scrap of paper scrawled with red ink; and the agile inventor had snatched it up almost as soon as the door flew open. He handed it to Angus without a word. The red ink on it actually was not dry, and the message ran, "If you have been to see her today, I shall kill you."

There was a short silence, and then Isidore Smythe said quietly, "Would you like a little whiskey? I rather feel as if I should."

"Thank you; I should like a little Flambeau," said Angus, gloomily. "This business seems to me to be getting rather grave. I'm going round at once to fetch him."

"Right you are," said the other, with admirable cheerfulness. "Bring him round here as quick as you can."

But as Angus closed the front door behind him he saw Smythe push back a button, and one of the clockwork images glided from its place and slid along a groove in the floor carrying a tray with syphon and decanter. There did seem something a trifle weird about leaving the little man alone among those dead servants, who were coming to life as the door closed.

Six steps down from Smythe's landing the man in shirt sleeves was doing something with a pail. Angus stopped to extract a promise, fortified with a prospective bribe, that he would remain in that place until the return with the detective, and would keep count of any kind of stranger coming up those stairs. Dashing down to the front hall he then laid similar charges of vigilance on the commissionaire at the front door, from whom he learned the simplifying circumstances that there was no back door. Not content with this, he captured the floating policeman and induced him to stand opposite the entrance and watch it; and finally paused an instant for a pennyworth of chestnuts, and an inquiry as to the probable length of the merchant's stay in the neighbourhood.

The chestnut seller, turning up the collar of his coat, told him he should probably be moving shortly, as he thought it was going to snow. Indeed, the evening was growing grey and bitter, but Angus, with all his eloquence, proceeded to nail the chestnut man to his post.

"Keep yourself warm on your own chestnuts," he said earnestly. "Eat up your whole stock; I'll make it worth your while. I'll give you a sovereign if you'll wait here till I come back, and then tell me whether any man, woman, or child has gone into that house where the commissionaire is standing."

He then walked away smartly, with a last look at the besieged tower.

"I've made a ring round that room, anyhow," he said. "They can't all four of them be Mr. Welkin's accomplices."

Lucknow Mansions were, so to speak, on a lower platform of that hill of houses, of which Himalayan Mansions might be called the peak. Mr. Flambeau's semi-official flat was on the ground floor, and presented in every way a marked contrast to the American machinery and cold hotel-like luxury of the flat of the Silent Service. Flambeau, who was a friend of Angus, received him in a rococo artistic den behind his office, of which the ornaments were sabres, harquebuses, Eastern curiosities, flasks of Italian wine, savage cooking-pots, a plumy Persian cat, and a small dusty-looking Roman Catholic priest, who looked particularly out of place.

"This is my friend Father Brown," said Flambeau. "I've often wanted you to meet him. Splendid weather, this; a little cold for Southerners like me."

"Yes, I think it will keep clear," said Angus, sitting down on a violet-striped Eastern ottoman.

"No," said the priest quietly, "it has begun to snow."

And, indeed, as he spoke, the first few flakes, foreseen by the man of chestnuts, began to drift across the darkening windowpane.

"Well," said Angus heavily. "I'm afraid I've come on business, and rather jumpy business at that. The fact is, Flambeau, within a stone's throw of your house is a fellow who badly wants your help; he's perpetually being haunted and threatened by an invisible enemy — a scoundrel whom nobody has even seen." As Angus proceeded to tell the whole tale of Smythe and Welkin, beginning with Laura's story, and going on with his own, the supernatural laugh at the corner of two empty streets, the strange distinct words spoken in an empty room, Flambeau grew more and more vividly concerned, and the little priest seemed to be left out of it, like a piece of furniture. When it came to the scribbled stamp-paper pasted on the window, Flambeau rose, seeming to fill the room with his huge shoulders.

"If you don't mind," he said, "I think you had better tell me the rest on the nearest road to this man's house. It strikes me, somehow, that there is no time to be lost."

"Delighted," said Angus, rising also, "though he's safe enough for the present, for I've set four men to watch the only hole to his burrow."

They turned out into the street, the small priest trundling after them with the docility of a small dog. He merely said, in a cheerful way, like one making conversation, "How quick the snow gets thick on the ground."

As they threaded the steep side streets already powdered with silver, Angus finished his story; and by the time they reached the crescent with the towering flats, he had leisure to turn his attention to the four sentinels. The chestnut seller, both before and after receiving a sovereign, swore stubbornly that he had watched the door and seen no visitor enter. The policeman was even more emphatic. He said he had had experience of crooks of all kinds, in top hats and in rags; he wasn't so green as to expect suspicious characters to look suspicious; he looked out for anybody, and, so help him, there had been nobody. And when all three men gathered round the gilded commissionaire, who still stood smiling astride of the porch, the verdict was more final still.

"I've got a right to ask any man, duke or dustman, what he wants in these flats," said the genial and gold-laced giant, "and I'll swear there's been nobody to ask since this gentleman went away."

The unimportant Father Brown, who stood back, looking modestly at the pavement, here ventured to say meekly, "Has nobody been up and down stairs, then, since the snow began to fall? It began while we were all round at Flambeau's."

"Nobody's been in here, sir, you can take it from me," said the official, with beaming authority.

"Then I wonder what that is?" said the priest, and stared at the ground blankly like a fish.

The others all looked down also; and Flambeau used a fierce exclamation and a French gesture. For it was unquestionably true that down the middle of the entrance guarded by the man in gold lace, actually between the arrogant, stretched legs of that colossus, ran a stringy pattern of grey footprints stamped upon the white snow.

"God!" cried Angus involuntarily, "the Invisible Man!"

Without another word he turned and dashed up the stairs, with Flambeau following; but Father Brown still stood looking about him in the snow-clad street as if he had lost interest in his query.

Flambeau was plainly in a mood to break down the door with his big shoulders; but the Scotchman, with more reason, if less intuition, fumbled about on the frame of the door till he found the invisible button; and the door swung slowly open.

It showed substantially the same serried interior; the hall had grown darker, though it was still struck here and there with the last crimson shafts of sunset, and one or two of the headless machines had been moved from their places for this or that purpose, and stood here and there about the twilight place. The green and red of their coats were all darkened in the dusk; and their likeness to human shapes slightly increased by their very shapelessness. But in the middle of them all, exactly where the paper with the red ink had lain, there lay something that looked like red ink spilt out of its bottle. But it was not red ink.

With a French combination of reason and violence Flambeau simply said "Murder!" and, plunging into the flat, had explored, every corner and cupboard of it in five minutes. But if he expected to find a corpse he found none. Isidore Smythe was not in the place, either dead or alive. After the most tearing search the two men met each other in the outer hall, with streaming faces and staring eyes. "My friend," said Flambeau, talking French in his excitement, "not only is your murderer invisible, but he makes invisible also the murdered man."

Angus looked round at the dim room full of dummies, and in some Celtic corner of his Scotch soul a shudder started. One of the life-size dolls stood immediately overshadowing the blood stain, summoned, perhaps, by the slain man an instant before he fell. One of the high-shouldered hooks that served the thing for arms, was a little lifted, and Angus had suddenly the horrid fancy that poor Smythe's own iron child had struck him down. Matter had rebelled, and these machines had killed their master. But even so, what had they done with him?

"Eaten him?" said the nightmare at his ear; and he sickened for an instant at the idea of rent, human remains absorbed and crushed into all that acephalous clockwork.

He recovered his mental health by an emphatic effort, and said to Flambeau, "Well, there it is. The poor fellow has evaporated like a cloud and left a red streak on the floor. The tale does not belong to this world."

"There is only one thing to be done," said Flambeau, "whether it belongs to this world or the other. I must go down and talk to my friend."

They descended, passing the man with the pail, who again asseverated that he had let no intruder pass, down to the commissionaire and the hovering chestnut man, who rigidly reasserted their own watchfulness. But when Angus looked round for his fourth confirmation he could not see it, and called out with some nervousness, "Where is the policeman?"

"I beg your pardon," said Father Brown; "that is my fault. I just sent him down the road to investigate something — that I just thought worth investigating."

"Well, we want him back pretty soon," said Angus abruptly, "for the wretched man upstairs has not only been murdered, but wiped out."

"How?" asked the priest.

"Father," said Flambeau, after a pause, "upon my soul I believe it is more in your department than mine. No friend or foe has entered the house, but Smythe is gone, as if stolen by the fairies. If that is not supernatural, I — "

As he spoke they were all checked by an unusual sight; the big blue policeman came round the corner of the crescent, running. He came straight up to Brown.

"You're right, sir," he panted, "they've just found poor Mr. Smythe's body in the canal down below."

Angus put his hand wildly to his head. "Did he run down and drown himself?" he asked.

"He never came down, I'll swear," said the constable, "and he wasn't drowned either, for he died of a great stab over the heart."

"And yet you saw no one enter?" said Flambeau in a grave voice.

"Let us walk down the road a little," said the priest.

As they reached the other end of the crescent he observed abruptly, "Stupid of me! I forgot to ask the policeman something. I wonder if they found a light brown sack."

"Why a light brown sack?" asked Angus, astonished.

"Because if it was any other coloured sack, the case must begin over again," said Father Brown; "but if it was a light brown sack, why, the case is finished."

"I am pleased to hear it," said Angus with hearty irony. "It hasn't begun, so far as I am concerned."

"You must tell us all about it," said Flambeau with a strange heavy simplicity, like a child.

Unconsciously they were walking with quickening steps down the long sweep of road on the other side of the high crescent, Father Brown leading briskly, though in silence. At last he said with an almost touching vagueness, "Well, I'm afraid you'll think it so prosy. We always begin at the abstract end of things, and you can't begin this story anywhere else.

"Have you ever noticed this — that people never answer what you say? They answer what you mean — or what they think you mean. Suppose one lady says to another in a country house, 'Is anybody staying with you?' the lady doesn't answer 'Yes; the butler, the three footmen, the parlourmaid, and so on,' though the parlourmaid may be in the room, or the butler behind her chair. She says 'There is nobody staying with us,' meaning nobody of the sort you mean. But suppose a doctor inquiring into an epidemic asks, 'Who is staying in the house?' then the lady will remember the butler, the parlourmaid, and the rest. All language is used like that; you never get a question answered literally, even when you get it answered truly. When those four quite honest men said that no man had gone into the Mansions, they did not really mean that no man had gone into them. They meant no man whom they could suspect of being your man. A man did go into the house, and did come out of it, but they never noticed him."

"An invisible man?" inquired Angus, raising his red eyebrows. "A mentally invisible man," said Father Brown.

A minute or two after he resumed in the same unassuming voice, like a man thinking his way. "Of course you can't think of such a man, until you do think of him. That's where his cleverness comes in. But I came to think of him through two or three little things in the tale Mr. Angus told us. First, there was the fact that this Welkin went for long walks. And then there was the vast lot of stamp paper on the window. And then, most of all, there were the two things the young lady said — things that couldn't be true. Don't get annoyed," he added hastily, noting a sudden movement of the Scotchman's head; "she thought they were true. A person can't be quite alone in a street a second before she receives a letter. She can't be quite alone in a street when she starts reading a letter just received. There must be somebody pretty near her; he must be mentally invisible."

"Why must there be somebody near her?" asked Angus.

"Because," said Father Brown, "barring carrier-pigeons, somebody must have brought her the letter."

"Do you really mean to say," asked Flambeau, with energy, "that Welkin carried his rival's letters to his lady?"

"Yes," said the priest. "Welkin carried his rival's letters to his lady. You see, he had to."

"Oh, I can't stand much more of this," exploded Flambeau. "Who is this fellow? What does he look like? What is the usual get-up of a mentally invisible man?"

"He is dressed rather handsomely in red, blue and gold," replied the priest promptly with precision, "and in this striking, and even showy, costume he entered Himalaya Mansions under eight human eyes; he killed Smythe in cold blood, and came down into the street again carrying the dead body in his arms — "

"Reverend sir," cried Angus, standing still, "are you raving mad, or am I?"

"You are not mad," said Brown, "only a little unobservant. You have not noticed such a man as this, for example."

He took three quick strides forward, and put his hand on the shoulder of an ordinary passing postman who had bustled by them unnoticed under the shade of the trees.

"Nobody ever notices postmen somehow," he said thoughtfully; "yet they have passions like other men, and even carry large bags where a small corpse can be stowed quite easily."

The postman, instead of turning naturally, had ducked and tumbled against the garden fence. He was a lean fair-bearded man of very ordinary appearance, but as he turned an alarmed face over his shoulder, all three men were fixed with an almost fiendish squint.

Flambeau went back to his sabres, purple rugs and Persian cat, having many things to attend to. John Turnbull Angus went back to the lady at the shop, with whom that imprudent young man contrives to be extremely comfortable. But Father Brown walked those snow-covered hills under the stars for many hours with a murderer, and what they said to each other will never be known.

THE UNFORGETTABLE NIGHT

It rained profusely for 3 days. Seema could hear the thunder and the shatters outside her house. The lightening passed through the glass pane into her living room as she sat beside the fire place involved in a book. The sudden thunder and lightning brought shivers in her as she woke up to close the shattering window. She peeped out to see the darkness stretched for miles apart. The trees were swaying from left to right enjoying the showers of the night. Darkness had engulfed the night along with the rain giving the night an eerie feel.

She sat alone by the fireplace on her chair rocking, feeling the coldness of the night. All of a sudden the powers went off, she was also engulfed in the pitch of darkness sending down shivers through her body. As she woke up to get the candle from the kitchen, her legs wouldn't move further, it was stuck there in fear of darkness. She brought in courage and moved forward humming a tune to herself to forget the fear that had fully engulfed her by now. With a mild light of her mobile phone she started looking out for the candle. her heart was pounding, she could hear them beat heavily and strongly than before, which gave her the feel that she was still alive.

Finally she had a sign of relief when she found the candle, she was about to light it when suddenly the phone rang, she gave a screech of fear throwing the candle away from her hand which she had found with a lot of difficulty. She picked the call and it was her mother on the other side. With a shaking voice she said, "Hello"- her mom asked her, " What happened," she told her that the power had gone and it had been raining here for 3 days making it difficult to move out of the house for the past 7 days.

She was a business woman and had been busy all the time. Since she was tired of her hectic life she thought she would take a break and spend her days in Ooty as she had hired a cottage to stay for a few days. Her mom was in London right now, she had gone there as her sister-in-law was delivering her first baby otherwise, her mom would have been with her here right now. This point of time Seema missed her a lot. She always had a phobia for darkness and it grew even more now.

The cottage was beautifully designed amidst a rubber estate. She usually hired a different cottage for the holidays but this time since this plan was made suddenly she could not avail that cottage so she had to take up this one. Her mom's call gave her a great sigh of relief and her fear had disappeared. She regained her strength again and searched for the candle and lit it.

She took the lighted candle in her hand and started moving to the living room. her shadow seemed larger than normal making her fear of her own self. She peeped out of the window; it was a full moon day. The scene outside looked awesome. The moon was smiling from between the trees which swayed heavily in the wind. The sound of the rain grew louder symbolizing that the rain had become heavier and it showed no signs of stopping, which meant that she would have to sit in the darkness for a longer time. She went back to sit near the fire place. Her own shadow was giving her fear. She just wanted to escape this fear so she decided to sleep with the hope that the rain would stop by the next day and she could go back home.

As she lay down on the couch within minutes she fell asleep. It was a loud screech which woke her up around midnight. The screeches brought in shivers to her. She opened her eyes and felt that it had stopped raining but it was still dark all over , she lighted the candle again and peeped out of the window and all she could hear were the dogs howling. She cursed them for howling at this time. Her heart beat grew louder, she could clearly hear each and every beat of it. Again a shrill sound of someone screeching loud reached her ears, her blood froze as if she was dreaming or was it real? No it was real, someone was screaming loud somewhere faraway. She trembled with fear. The sound of the dogs howling brought her sweats even on a cold night.

She ran back to the couch, pulled her bed sheet up and lay down trying to forget the fear but it was not going to leave her. The shreak grew louder and more intense. She started to tremble, she could feel huge beads of sweat running down her forehead. Her heart was beating faster now. She felt that her heart would stop beating now if it ran so fast. She picked up the courage and slowly walked towards the window and moved the curtains to peep out.

Her heart missed a beat and she gave a louder shreak than the one she had heard before. The powers came on at the same time, maybe god had sensed that if he left her like this anymore she would die of fear. A girl was standing just outside her window blood stained. Her blood became cold, she froze at this sight. No she could not move, she was so much in fear that her mind had switched off, she remembered the stories her colleagues had told her before she booked the cottage.

They had told her that a young girl had been murdered brutally by her landlord and that her ghost was still there roaming awaiting his arrival to revenge on him. Many people who had stayed in this cottage had told that they had heard the screams and shouts of a girl faraway and they believed that the blood stained girl even kept knocking at the door sometimes crying for help. And after many such incidents people stopped renting this cottage, which was why she could find this cottage at a very reasonable rate. She never believed in ghosts and all these stories just seemed funny to her, and she laughed and made fun of them. This was one of the reasons why she took up this cottage and challenged to stay alone here to show everyone that ghosts do not exist. She now thought that she was a fool and she had encountered a ghost and thAT ghosts do exist. How can she not believe she had really seen the girl right in front of her.

She gathered courage and moved to the couch and sat there reciting some prayers. She had heard that when she recited prayers ghosts didn't attack . She could still hear her screams and shouts. She closed her ears and sat. She was shivering literally now. No not because of the cold but because of fear, The clock struck one, she could hear the sound of the clock ticking along with the beats of her heart. Thud !Thud! Thud! No they were not her heart beats but someone banging on her door loudly. As they had told her it was the girl who was banging her door crying for help. She froze thinking that the ghost was not going to leave her . She ran and sat under the table as if the ghost was playing hide and seek with her . When one is engulfed in fear the master of our body, which makes human beings superior to animals gets switched off and does things which sound really funny when you think about it later.

She sat under the table thinking that the ghost won't be able to find her immediately in case it entered the house through the door like they show in movies. Thoughts go weird when you are scared. The most brilliant men like Einstein would also think such things when in fear. She was thinking of ways to escape from the ghost but no way was she going to leave her. The bangs grew louder indicating that she was still waiting outside. She sat under the table for almost an hour waiting for her to leave. Slowly in a few hours the bangs stopped giving her a great sigh of relief. She gathered strength and switched on the lights of all the rooms assuming that ghosts don't attack when in bright light. After a long and deep thinking she gathered her mental and physical strength and planned to open the door to check out if she had left.

She walked slowly to the door, opened it a little bit and found that no one was there. Then her fear disappeared. She opened the door wide and moved out to see if she (ghost) had really left. She suddenly tripped over something and fell. To her shock she found a girl lying there on the floor. She screamed with fear and went near her slowly to see if she was a ghost, no she was not, she was just a human being like her . She was badly hurt and that was why she was bleeding badly. She felt ashamed of her stupidity. She lifted her to her house and tried waking her. She splashed water to wake her up, she woke up stunned and started crying pleading to help her or else she would be killed.

She calmed her down, gave her some water and also first aid for her wounds and then something to eat. Now she listened to her story. She said she was kidnapped by a few people and there was a gang of people for that, who kidnap children and send them for begging and earn money through them, if they do not abide by what they say they would be brutally beaten up. She was the prey to them today and was beaten up just because she refused to do what they wanted.

So this made her realize that the shreak which the people used to hear in this cottage was coming from there and not a ghost as all the people there had thought. They refused to open their doors fearing that it could be the ghost when they heard cries of help. If they would have done it then they could have saved many innocent children like her. She looked very scared and innocent. She told her not to get scared and that she would save her from their clutches and also the other children who were there.

Seema immediately called the police and they reached her cottage around 4 in the morning. The girl recited the entire story to them and the police nabbed the gang of 5 and also rescued the small innocent children from their clutches. The police congratulated Seema for her braveness and said that they would award her for her brave work from the government.

Only you and she know the story of her braveness so let's keep it within us as a secret forever!!!!!!

THE END